# The Book of
# Masks

## Stories by Hwang Sun-won

Edited with an Introduction by
Martin Holman

readers international

Published in English by Readers International Inc., and Readers
International, London. Editorial inquiries to London office at
8 Strathray Gardens, London NW3 4NY England. US/Canadian
inquiries to Subscriber Service Department, P.O. Box 959,
Columbia LA 71418−0959 USA.

*A Numerical Enigma, For Dear Life* and *The Night He Came Late*
reprinted with kind permission of the translators. *The Weighted
Tumbler* reprinted with kind permission of *Korea Journal*.
Cover art: *Self Portrait* by Yun Du-so (1668-1715), in collection of Mr
Yun Young-son, used courtesy of National Museum of Korea.
Design by Jan Brychta
Typesetting by Opus 43, Cumbria, UK

**Printed in Malta by Interprint Limited.**

*Library of Congress Catalog Card Number:* 88-63251

*British Library Cataloguing in Publication Data*

Hwang, Sun-won
  The Book of Masks
  1.Short Stories in Korean 1945- English Text
  I. Title II. Holman, Martin
  895.7'34 [F]

ISBN 0-930523-57-1 hardcover
ISBN 0-930523-58-X paperback

# Contents

*Introduction* by Martin Holman ......................................v

*Masks* ........................................................... xv

Conversation in June about Mothers........................... 1

A Numerical Enigma......................................... 6

Winter Forsythias.............................................21

Folding the Umbrella........................................35

For Dear Life ................................................43

Blood .......................................................55

The Night He Came Late ...................................68

In a Small Island Village....................................85

Shadows of a Sound ........................................93

The Weighted Tumbler ....................................102

Nature......................................................118

The Curtain Fell, but Then ................................141

Places of Death............................................154

A Tree, a Rock and.........................................168

# Introduction
by Martin Holman

Hwang Sun-won began his literary career 58 years ago with the publication of his first poem when he was 16. In the years since, he has distinguished himself as a poet, a novelist, and a writer of short stories in his native Korea, where his name is a household word. He has written over 100 short stories, which appeared in eight collections published from the nineteen thirties to the mid-seventies. He produced two volumes of poetry early in his career, and also has authored seven novels, including his *Trees on a Cliff* (translated into English by Chang Wang-rok) and *The Moving Castle* (translated into English by Bruce and Ju-chan Fulton), both of which won major literary awards in Korea. Today, at the age of 74, Hwang still writes and teaches creative writing.

When Hwang was born in 1915 in what is now North Korea, his nation had already been under Japanese rule for five years. In the late nineteenth century, as the five hundred-year-old Yi Dynasty of Korea began to feel the pressure of encroachment by Western forces, Japan positioned itself to annex Korea in a move to procure colonies after the fashion of Western powers. By 1910 the Japanese had acquired enough influence in Korea to take over the country, thus beginning 35 years of colonial occupation.

Under colonial rule, Korean children were educated in Japanese schools, part of an effort to "assimilate"

Korea into the expanding Japanese empire. Attempts to turn Koreans into Japanese took many forms; at various times such "subversives" as the compilers of a Korean language dictionary, those who opposed Japanese rule, and many others were subjected to imprisonment and torture for what was viewed as Korean nationalistic activities. At one point Koreans were even required to give up their Korean names and adopt Japanese ones. Hwang was educated and did his early writing under these adverse conditions. For his higher education he went to Japan, graduating with a degree in English Literature from Waseda University in Tokyo in 1939.

In Japan, Hwang was exposed to the very active literary world of Tokyo in the 1930s when such young, prominent Japanese writers as Kawabata Yasunari and Tanizaki Jun'ichiro were active. Hwang's experience in Japan gave him an opportunity to sharpen his vision and view his own culture from afar. But when he returned to Korea after the completion of his degree, he found Japanese control growing tighter. Eventually Hwang went into hiding to avoid conscription by the occupation authorities. In 1942, the Japanese outlawed all publication in the Korean language as their Pacific war efforts expanded. During the subsequent years before the liberation of Korea with the Japanese surrender in 1945, Hwang and other Korean authors continued to write secretly with the uncertain hope that their works would one day see the light of day.

Before the liberation, resistance movements, both nationalist and Marxist, had already developed among the Koreans. The 38th parallel was originally chosen merely as a boundary to facilitate division of the responsibilities of the United States and the Soviet Union in accepting the surrender of Japanese troops on the peninsula; however, the line soon hardened into an ideological boundary. Hwang's home had been in the North where he had hoped to remain, but the tyranny and terror of the communists prompted him to flee to the South with his family in 1946.

When the Korean War broke out in 1950, many Koreans fled before the advancing communist army which soon occupied the entire peninsula except for an area around the southern port city of Pusan. Hwang and his family spent much of the war as refugees here while the war front swept back up and down the peninsula, ravaging a nation that had already been plundered by thirty-five years of foreign occupation. South Korea was assisted by United Nations forces, while the North was eventually joined by the Chinese army. By the time an uneasy peace settled over the land in 1953, hundreds of thousands of Koreans on both sides had lost their lives, farms and industries had been destroyed, and the 38th parallel still divided the Korean people. The war and partitioning of Korea separated hundreds of thousands of families, many of whom are only now being reunited from their scattered locations within South Korea, not to mention those whose relatives live in the North beyond the demilitarized zone, who hold little hope of being reunited.

Recovery from the Korean War – political, economic, spiritual, and emotional – has been a painful process. The first government of South Korea instituted after the liberation war was racked by corruption and was toppled in part by the success of the April 19 student revolution of 1960, which chrystallized public sentiment against the regime of President Syngman Rhee. The democracy that followed Rhee was short-lived; General Park Chunghee took power in a military coup that lasted until his assassination in 1979. This period saw rapid industrial growth, but inequalities of wealth left many Koreans out of the nation's economic advancement.

In 1988, Korea became the focus of world attention when Seoul hosted the Olympics, as well as many other international events, including the International P.E.N. Congress. Most Koreans are justifiably proud of the progress they have made as a nation; and, while there appears to be guarded but growing optimism, grave problems still trouble the Korean people: reunification is still a major preoccupation, however unlikely the prospects appear; labour unrest and government responses to it threaten the stability of the industries that have spawned the so-called economic miracle of this "little tiger" nation; the desire for expanded personal freedom often seems to run counter to the demands of national security.

Hwang has lived in or around Seoul, the center of modern Korean culture, since the end of the Korean War. In his life, which spans the great portion of modern Korean history, he has witnessed the myriad political, social, and economic changes that have come over his country, but his literature can be said to reflect those changes only in an oblique fashion. Hwang's literature does not so much depict his society as it does the individuals' reactions – often very personal ones – to it. Hwang has never made his own politics a matter of literary record nor has he ever affiliated himself with any of the many literary movements that aroused the passion and claimed the devotion of some Korean writers in this century. Such writers as Yi Kwang-su, who wrote what is considered Korea's first modern novel, *Heartlessness*, regarded literature as a tool to educate and enlighten the people in a modernizing society, and for some time in the 1920s a debate raged between Yi and Kim Tong-in, whose hedonistic lifestyle and insistence on art for art's sake were in direct opposition to Yi's views. Proletarian writers also appeared, but they fared poorly under Japanese oppression, as did any writers who dared to criticize the colonial regime. And since the liberation of 1945, most literary movements of the West have found voices in Korea as well. In recent years, Hwang's literature has come to be regarded as unresponsive to the needs of a rapidly developing society by some who follow younger, so-called socially committed writers. But Hwang's literature does not evade the problems of society; it recognizes and explores the constants in man's reaction to society, and those constants involve the universal workings of the soul.

Through almost six decades of writing, something central to Hwang's work has remained unchanged: his devotion to his art coupled with a devotion to his subject, human life. Prof. Suh Ji-moon of Korea University in Seoul, some of whose translations appear in this book, has described Hwang's literary demeanor as being a product of his "aestheticism and asceticism." She describes his aestheticism as "a rigorous search for exactly the right form to convey his meaning and a disciplined quest for the image that encapsulates a whole personality, emotional complex, or historical heritage. Thus it is inseparable from his asceticism." Hwang has not ignored his time in his literature, although there was often little other choice during the Japanese occupation, a time when the literature of Korea makes conspicuously little mention of the Japanese, and opposition appears only in veiled references. His characters *do* confront the political and social problems of their age; the wounded young man in "For Dear Life" has participated in the April 19 student revolution that brought the downfall of the Rhee government, and the schizophrenic narrator of "A Numerical Enigma" also takes up his role in the movement. But Hwang has chosen to deal with those characters in a manner that transcends time as well as place. Their reactions to their world are personal, not public, and they lead toward universal themes that are immediately comprehensible across time and from East to West.

Hwang's literature takes up questions that touch all people everywhere: among others, human loneliness and the passage of time, the loss of innocence, and the uneasy distance between men and women. While these inherent problems of existence have led some writers to despair, there is a strong moral under-pinning to Hwang's work that suggests hope, resolution, and meaning. Hwang often portrays characters who are lonely and isolated, but ultimately he shifts his focus on their lives from the bleak emptiness they often experience to the exquisite nature of their moments of juncture. In his 1958 story

"Ringwanderung" (the title, a German word, refers to the tendency of a hiker without any kind of guide to veer consistently in a circle unaware of his deviation), Hwang compares the lonely wandering of humans through life to travel along the remote reaches of a lonely circle. But the desolation is not his emphasis.

> Surely the two of us had been wandering unknowingly in circles. When wandering in a circle, some people go left while others go right. . . . But in *Ringwanderung*, the most important thing – more than anything else – is the moment when the two circles meet.

Hwang's focus is the point of juncture, of communication.

Often this intersection involves reaching across the years to ignite a spark of contact that gives significance to his characters' lives and rescues them from dark loneliness. In "Old Man Hwang", a story written in 1942 and loosely based on Hwang's own grandfather, a self-reliant widower farmer tries to shun festivities that have been prepared for his own sixtieth birthday celebration. When an itinerant musician appears at his gate hoping to be hired to entertain, the farmer recognizes him as a boyhood freind, long forgotten, and they share wine and memories, away from the noisy gaiety of his neighbors who are celebrating without him. They sit in the shadows in a room together and return to their youth, sharing wine in a communion with their past.

The narrator of "Shadows of a Sound," in the present volume, makes a connection with his past, though this must come from beyond death. Perplexed by his inability to grasp something of substance from what he sees now as a grown man on his return to his childhood home town, the man is touched from the past and transformed in a peculiar, private way by a long forgotten boyhood friend who is now dead.

The loss of innocence figures as a concern in a number of Hwang's stories. In "Blood," in this collection, a father discovers the mercantile blood-thirstiness his six-year-old son has learned, even as the father finds himself victimized by others. Hwang's best-known story in Korea, "The Cloudburst" ("The Shower" in some translations), written in 1952, which depicts a young country boy and a girl recently moved from the city, is widely regarded as a portrait of puppy love, the pure relationship of children. However, disturbing, ominous images surround the two: the clear, gentle stream they had crossed on the way out on a walk through the countryside grows turbid and raging on their return after a sudden shower forced them to seek shelter in a field.

The city girl in "The Cloudburst" is also an example of the powerful women, often worldy-wise, who appear in a number of Hwang's stories. "The Night He Came Late," "Conversation in June About Mothers," and "The Curtain Fell, but Then . . ." all demonstrate a mystical feminine power that begins with the preeminence of the image of mother, an image that colors or twists all subsequent male-female relations.

The stories in *The Book of Masks* are all drawn from Hwang's last collection of short stories, which was published in 1976 under the title *T'al* (Masks). The stories, written between 1965 and 1975, take up themes familiar to readers of his earlier work and show the insight and incisiveness of the masterful hand of mature experience.

Hwang's choice of "Masks" as the title story for his last collection is significant. Masks appear in most cultures of the world and serve a variety of purposes. The mask may be used to conceal or to change identities. It may be considered a work of art in itself, or perform a dramatic role on stage. Perhaps the most common function of the mask lies in religious ritual where, rather than concealment, its purpose is revelation.

Masks are seldom intended to be realistic portraits, except for the death masks of Europe that were meant to reproduce accurately the features of the deceased; most masks are stylized conceptions of their models. The mask presents the distillation, the essence of the subject, often supernatural. The power of the mask lies in its ability to link two worlds: the sacred and the profane, the young and the old, the living and the dead. The maker of masks is revered in many cultures for his ability to give physical form to the essence of the subject, a capacity that suggests he is in contact with the supernatural.

As a maker of "masks," Hwang strives to draw together the local and the universal. His stories are firmly rooted in the soil of his native Korea, but they are immediately comprehensible and moving for readers far removed from the source. Although his settings and situations are peculiar to this nation in this northeast corner of Asia, his concerns are the concerns of all humanity.

In the story "Masks," the young soldier is depicted

as passing through several incarnations, each unique, but each connected to and dependent on the others. Hwang links the soldier back to the soil, plants, and animals of his youth on the farm, and ultimately, and ironically, to the soldier's own killer, a fellow Korean, now a suffering veteran of the war. Beneath the multitude of masks – and the masks of the multitude – Hwang has sought the bonds that join together the people of his divided land as Koreans and fellow human beings.

Each of these stories may be considered a "mask" in that it presents an aspect, a visage, of human experience. Rather than paint an elaborate mural, Hwang uses simple evocative strokes in each story to depict the essence of the heart, to create a message that reaches across the gulf that separates us. Hwang Sun-won has stated that a writer's task is not only to discover beauty, but to seek the salvation of man. In his literature, Hwang approaches this labor aware of the loneliness, depravity, squalor, and brutality in the soul of man, but, recognizing that there is also great strength and virtue in the heart and human bonds, he strives to forge the links that save the human spirit from the void.

*Berkeley, February 1989*

# Masks

*Wounded by a bullet in the leg, the soldier fell. As he tried to lift himself, a bayonet pierced his chest. In the instant he lost consciousness, the face of his attacker was imprinted on his eyes as though burned there. The blood from the soldier's chest flowed into the yellow earth of this desolate battlefield. It was at the foot of a hill far from his home, yet it resembled the land around his own village.*

His blood soaked into the earth and became earth. The dead soldier had been a farmer, and for him soil was life itself. At first this soil was a deeper shade than the rest, but gradually it became all one color.

The roots of a purple eulalia reed furtively sipped the soldier's life, and he became reed.

A jumble of combat boots trampled the reed and moved on. In winter, boots heavier than before trod upon the snow-covered reed. Time after time they trampled it and left, but the plant did not die. After the boots had moved on, the reed was blown by the breezes in spring, bathed in sunbeams, washed by rain and dew, covered with snow, and blown once again by the spring breezes. In the late spring the reed was cut down by a farmer's scythe and carried to a stable.

Here the reed became a bull. Just as the dead man had done when he was a farmer, the bull's owner cared for it as if it were the most important member of his family. Now the soldier worked hard alongside the farmer. He *worked until his skin was bruised and swollen, but keeping the farm alive from year to year was not easy. Then a flood swept away the fields, and one night that autumn the farmer stifled the sound of his own crying as he stroked the scruff of the soldier's neck. The soldier passed through the market, then went by train to the slaughterhouse. He was hung up in a butcher's in the city, where meat was cut and sold from his carcass. There he saw someone he knew — the one who had pierced his chest with a bayonet at the foot of the hill. He was begging for food. He ate a piece of the meat from scraps he had begged at a restaurant, and the soldier entered this man.*

*The man tossed away his empty begging tin and hoisted himself up, one sleeve of his worn-out work clothes dangling where he had no arm. He went toward the iron foundry where he had worked as a lathe operator before the war took his arm. He strode inside and approached his former boss.*

*"Good day."*

*The foundry master's face showed his displeasure. He crushed out his cigarette with the toe of his shoe.*

*"Don't worry, I haven't come here to badger you, sir. I've come here to work as I did before."*

*The master cast an uncomfortable glance at the armless sleeve.*

*"What are you looking at?" The man eyed the master squarely and continued, "I was wounded in the leg by a bullet, but does that mean I can't operate a lathe?"*

*The man shifted his body as he spoke, his empty sleeve dangling at his side.*

*Translated by Martin Holman*

# Conversation in June about Mothers

We were lounging on grass, with the hot sun of June pouring on our backs. Traffic noise drifting from the nearby street intruded from time to time on our conversation.

"My wife had just given birth, and it was a difficult birth, too, so there was no way she could flee to the South with us. So we decided that I would leave with our eleven-year-old son, our eldest, and come back later to fetch my wife, our seven-year-old son, and the new baby. Of course, we didn't know at the time that the 38th parallel was soon going to be completely impassable.

"My eldest son used to be a daddy's boy. He slept in my bed from the day he was weaned. And he followed me wherever I went. He even cried out 'Daddy' when he fell down or got hurt or something, at those times when other children cry out 'Mommy', you know. All my neighbors called him 'Daddy's boy.'

"Well, he willingly consented to go with me and he shouldered his backpack and prepared to leave without any hesitation. When my wife told him to be sure to hold onto my hand tightly and to be especially careful not to let go in crowded places and dark alleys, he smiled and told her not to worry. He looked so mature that I was proud and felt as if I had a grown-up companion for the difficult journey.

"My wife saw us off, simply standing at the gate. I walked on without looking back at her, and my son walked in front of me, also without looking back.

"We were just about to turn the corner and disappear from my wife's sight when she suddenly called my son. And look at what this boy did.

"He had been walking ahead as if going with me and leaving his mother behind was the most natural thing in the world, when he stopped dead on hearing his mother's voice, as if his feet had frozen to the ground. Then my wife's voice sounded again, 'Stay with me, dearest,' and my son sprang off and ran back towards the house. He didn't give me so much as a sidelong glance. And he was the boy everybody believed was more fond of me than of her.

"He'd have been a great comfort to me if he had come along. But I don't blame him. On the contrary, the more I think of it, the more I think he acted beautifully."

I commented, playfully, "What an insignificant father you must have been, to be deserted by your son that way."

My friend, now in his early fifties, spoke somewhat sadly but firmly. "No. A mother is an absolute being. Compared to a mother, a father means nothing. That's an unalterable truth."

"You think so?" Another man, the youngest in the group, said rather querulously. All eyes turned toward him. "Do you really think a mother is an absolute being? My mother eloped with a lover when

I was seven years old. In other words, she deserted me." He paused a little and then continued.

"The only memory I have of my mother is waking up frightened one night and asking her to light the lamp, and her not doing it."

"Maybe there was a black-out," someone suggested.

"I wish it was that. But the fact was, my mother had a lover. My father was often absent from home on account of his business. So my mother got herself a lover, and finally ran away with him, deserting me."

"You didn't see her at all after that?"

"No. She never came to see me, and I didn't try to find her. Why should I look for her? I have nothing but hatred for her."

"You sound pretty bitter about it."

"Yeah. As a soldier I was severely wounded during the War. It was the thick of battle and there was no telling when the medics would arrive. My wound hurt terribly, and I was bleeding hard. My consciousness was growing dim and I thought I was going to die. At that moment, out of nowhere, I saw my mother's face. But I rejected her. I rejected her concern even on the brink of death."

"How did you know the face was your mother's, if she left you when you were seven?"

"It's true I don't remember her face, and I never even tried to dig up her picture to see what she looked like. But somehow, I knew it was my mother. I can't explain it."

"That's understandable," someone commented.

"And her face was peculiar, too. She was holding out her tongue. And I knew instantly why."

We all waited in silence for his explanation.

"Once, when I was very little I had sore eyes. In the morning my eyes were glued tight with mucus, and my mother licked them open for me. I had not recalled the incident at all until then, but the moment I saw my mother's face with her tongue out, I remembered. Then I told myself that I must not close my eyes and allow my mother to lick them open with her hateful tongue. I kept thinking that to myself until I lost consciousness."

"Then, couldn't you say that thought kept you alive? It seems to me that your mother saved your life after all," I commented.

"For me, the important thing is that I tried to keep my eyes open to reject her help. I don't think it's important that I stayed alive. In any case, I rejected my mother, and I still don't think mothers are absolute beings."

"But it seems to prove that deep down in your subconscious you yearned for her."

"Do you think so? I don't. I . . . I really don't know."

For a moment doubt flitted across his eyes. Then he concluded. "I don't know whether mothers are absolute beings or not, but I do think there's something mysterious about them."

Another man was telling his story.

"On the night we fled to the South, there was thick fog on the shore of Imjin River. In dead silence our party boarded the small boat waiting for us. We were all trying to escape communist rule in the North. The only way we could reach freedom was if we could cross the river safely.

"The boatman rowed as silently as possible. But

from time to time the oars grated against the side of the boat, and everybody winced. Even the water slapping the sides of the boat made us uneasy. We all held our breath.

"When the boat reached the middle of the river, the fog lifted and stars began to appear in the sky. Everybody was afraid that the boat might be spotted by the shore guard. That would mean the end of us all.

"Right then, a baby began to cry. Its voice was so shrill and loud, everyone was terrified. But immediately the crying stopped. The mother had thrown the baby into the water. There was a splash and then silence again.

"We crossed the river safely."

Someone commented, "When it comes to questions of life and death, even maternal instinct gives way to the instinct for self-preservation. You can't blame her."

But I didn't agree. I thought the woman deserved to be cursed and spat upon. However, I kept my silence.

"The mother's breasts got swollen with milk," the man went on with his story. It occurred to me that the woman might have been this man's wife.

"I suppose she had a hard time squeezing out all that milk?" I said, rather sarcastically.

"She didn't squeeze it out. She cut off both her nipples with scissors . . . with her own hands," the man said slowly.

The afternoon sun of June was still tingling on our backs.

*Translated by Suh Ji-moon*

# A Numerical Enigma

I'd like to talk to you because I think you would understand what I want to say. The basic cause of it all was the color of my face, and the thing that set it off was that woman. She lives in the same public housing building as I do. I live on the fifth floor and she's on the fourth. It's been about a month and a half since I came to know that she and I live in the same building. I haven't any idea whether she moved in about that time or whether I just didn't know until then that she was living there. But I even know that she lives at the end of the left side on the fourth floor.

That woman and I see each other just about every day. It's when I'm on my way home after work and she's on her way out that we meet, either on the stairs of the apartment building or perhaps on the way up the street next to the apartment house in front of some shop or office. I don't know what she does, but she goes out at the same time that I come home from the office. She always wears a Korean-style dress. She has a smallish face with big eyes and doesn't use much make-up. She gives a fresh and neat impression.

One day I met this woman on the street at the foot of the hill, right by the place where the old men with nothing to do sit and operate their little neighborhood broker's office. That day she was wearing light green clothes. But she wasn't alone. Another young woman about the same age was with her, wearing western-style clothing.

I'm not sure when it began, but whenever I met this woman I avoided her gaze as though there were some kind of problem. In fact, every time we passed, the woman would also modestly lower her head. It would happen every time. Then I began to think quite differently about our responses to each other. After all, is it so unusual for a man and a woman to sense this kind of subtle feeling? Day by day that feeling seemed to be increasing. All the while I waited for some chance to get closer to this woman.

Then it became clear one day that my hopes had been vain after all. I was on my way up the street, and the woman was on her way out. The distance separating us was shrinking and we were just about to pass, the woman with her head modestly bowed, and I avoiding her eyes. She was whispering something to the other young woman with her. Then the two women started to giggle, trying as best they could to keep from laughing.

I wasn't able to hear what it was that the woman had been whispering, because her voice was so low. But I knew anyway. I could tell why it was that the two of them tried to hold back their laughter. Suddenly I felt hot all over. I was certain that they were laughing about my complexion. I felt flustered and began to walk away. I had only one idea, to put distance between me and that woman as fast as I could.

What did you say? That it's good to have a

complexion that's naturally fair? You're just trying to make me feel better. But it happens that I don't like the pale color of my face. And it's not just my own face, either. I can't stand anything white. White always makes me feel uneasy. It actually frightens me when I think that white has the power to absorb all other colors, to the point where it seems as though no color could ever complete or satisfy it. How easily I could even wish these bandages on my forehead could become red, completely soaked in blood. I'm lucky that the sheets on this bed are blue. What a relief it would be if these white walls too, could be painted black.

Anyway, it seems as though my white face has wrecked everything for me. My student days were the really decisive time. Once and for all I lost the chance to see whether I might have been able to get out from under the burden of this white complexion. Perhaps I hesitated before the infinite possibility, or more likely I was afraid, but it was over before I realized what had happened.

It was the same with the woman. That day I somehow had to show my face to her. I had to force the issue. Was I going to be able to win her acceptance, or was I going to merit only her reproach? It seems I forfeited my opportunity all over again.

I came back to the apartment and went to my own room. My younger brother and I were sharing it. I took hold of the knob and opened the door. I had barely put a foot inside when I backed out and shut the door again. A tall black figure was occupying the center of the room. In the moment the door was open, it seemed as though the thief had expanded and was filling all the space in the room. I wished that someone would come and chase this person out, but I could hardly call the old woman who lived next door. So there was nothing to do but sit down in the hall and wait until my brother came back. My kid brother was attending college at the time.

After a long while he came back. I whispered to him what had happened. I asked him when he went in to chase away the person who was there. For some time already my brother had been cold and distant toward me. He looked at me for a moment with a disdainful expression, then he went into the room without saying a word. A long time went by and there wasn't a sign of the black figure's leaving or any word from my brother. I couldn't wait any longer and very quietly opened the door. But what do you suppose? There was my brother all alone, lying on the floor with his head in his arm, smoking a cigarette. I asked where the person had gone. Without a word my brother glared at me.

How in the world could that black figure have slipped away? There wasn't another door to the place besides the one to the hall where I had come in. He would have to go that way, but I hadn't seen a thing. After all, I had been waiting there the whole time for my brother. If the figure hadn't left by the door, then he had to go out through the window or pass right through the wall itself. I thought probably that's what the black figure would have done. I asked my brother whether he had taken anything. He simply stared at me vacantly. I looked all around the room.

Aha, something was missing after all. Everyth else was in place, but the calendar that h hanging on the wall had unaccountabl

I asked my brother whether the black thief hadn't taken the calendar. Only then did he finally speak, and then with the insolent retort, "Didn't you take it down yourself and burn it just a few days ago?"

"What nonsense! When did I ever take down that calendar and burn it? That black figure took it. Instead of allowing my death to be postponed, they've confiscated all my allotted time."

I was angry at my brother, who didn't see this at all and just lay there stupidly. "A young punk like you shouldn't just hang around the house. Even if you don't have any work to do, you could at least go out and swill down some cheap wine!"

I stuck my hand in my pocket and threw at my brother what money was there. But I really wasn't angry at him so much as at myself. I was taking it out on my brother for nothing, just because at that time the memory of my own student days was on my mind.

Something else happened just before that. It was a Saturday, so I had finished work at the office early and was on the way home. I was walking toward the bus stop when suddenly the brilliant sunlight was all shattered. A bicycle going by in the street fell over, and all the glass bottles that had been stacked on the back of it were smashed. All those tiny fragments of glass in the street were reflecting the light. It was a glorious sight. As if to spite the poor errand boy looking down at them with a discouraged expression, those broken pieces kept on sending out their brilliant, changing colors. Only there was one bit of glass that was in a state of dark death. That particle was separated from the others. It had lost its light; it had been extinguished had become a part of the dark asphalt pavement.

That was exactly how the time of my disgrace came in April 1960. Turning my back on the knotted procession choking the streets, I broke ranks and sat in a corner of my room, going from bad to worse. The April 19th Revolution and my downfall hung in the balance together.

I don't know when it started, but I began the habit of thinking of the 9 in the date April 19 as being changed into a 6. I'm sure you will agree that of all the numbers, 6 and 9 are the most intriguing. Turn 9 upside down and you get a 6, or turn a 6 over and it becomes a 9. No, what you should say is, straighten up a 9 and it becomes a 6, or straighten up a 6 and it's really a 9.

Now the other numbers aren't like that, are they? You invert them and they're nothing. Except of course for the number 8, which keeps its own form whether you turn it over or leave it as it is.

Anyway, when I see a 9, it just seems to me like a 6 that got turned over by mistake, and when I see a 6, it always looks like a 9 written upside down by mistake. So 9's have to be corrected to 6's, and 6's are right only when they are corrected to be 9's.

Do I really think that is correcting them? Oh, yes, it certainly is. How did my otherwise logical mind get involved in a confusion like this, you say? This is no confusion. What I'm saying is absolutely right. That's why you have to correct April 19, 1960 so that it becomes April 16, 1690.

And that's not all. Not long ago I began to correct all the mistakes in the records of the company where I work. That means fixing the 9's into 6's and the 6's into 9's. My section chief warned me not to, but I still went ahead and did it the way I believe it should be done. Someday the section chief is going to realize that what I did was the right thing. No question about it, that time will come. It's really difficult to live alone like this, surrounded by all these people who don't understand.

Don't I have any close friends? Of course I do, why not? I have college classmates and people I work with at the office. Just the same, it's been a long time since I've met my friends. When I meet them we find we simply don't have anything in common to talk about. The things they get all worked up over and talk about just don't get my interest up at all. So what if I think it's better to spend my time by myself? It's such a nuisance to try to talk to the people at the office that I can sometimes go for days at a time without saying a word.

And yet somehow today, as I told you a while ago, I thought you would understand me, so I feel free to open up and talk to you like this.

Gradually I wanted more and more to be by myself. This didn't cause me any distress or inconvenience at all. Didn't I go to work? I decided to take off from work at the office until they could really understand why it was that I had to change all the 9's and 6's that were wrong. In the end – and it was by my own choice – I came to spend nearly all the twenty-four hours of each day alone. Mind you, this is what I wanted.

Now, while I was passing my time alone like this, I don't know why but I found myself concentrating repeatedly upon certain words. *Love* and then *sacrifice*, these were the two words. How meaningful and beautiful these words are! Then one day after I had been turning these words over and over again in my mind, I was struck by an idea that took me completely by surprise. It was that, while I couldn't get these precious and beautiful words out of my mind, I discovered that I myself was pursuing their exact opposites. That made me feel somehow I had an obligation to get them – even though I didn't know just what they were – out in the open. But I was unable to figure out exactly what those opposites might be.

That was several days ago; to be precise, it was four days and eighteen hours ago. Finally something happened that made me realize what they were. I had gone out in the afternoon and walked around the neighborhood to get some fresh air. Those days I had consciously been walking around the neighborhood at hours that were different from my usual commuting routine, so I would avoid seeing that woman.

That day I left the apartment house at about three in the afternoon, and when I had gone about half way down the steep street, I came across a boy of five or six who was fighting with a girl about the same age. The girl was going after him, yelling something, and the boy had backed off and wasn't able to get a word in edgewise. The girl went after the boy more and more vigorously, but he was too slow in backing up, so finally she nearly ran right into him.

When that happened the boy stuck out his hands as if to defend himself from the girl, and touched the front of the old dress she was wearing. At that point the girl put up her arms, clasped her breasts, sat down on the spot and burst out bawling. The boy hadn't shoved her, and he hadn't grabbed at her clothes or anything like that, either. He drew back again the way he had before, then spun around and ran down the side road nearby.

I think it's possible in this world to receive

intimations even from the most insignificant incidents, don't you? As I stood looking at the place where the girl sat crying after the boy had left, the thing I had been searching for, almost as a kind of duty, came to me in a very clear way. I experienced the most delicious feeling of joy at the thought that if I could just put this idea into practice, everything would be a success.

But then as I began to walk again, the black figure stood defying me, blocking the way. I don't know why, but I wasn't afraid of him. I just stood and looked directly at him without moving. It looked for a moment as though he was going to spread and grow large, but then all of a sudden he feebly shrank away and disappeared.

When did I first start seeing this black figure? I can still remember it exactly. The first time I encountered the thief was during my senior year in college. It was on the day when a notice suddenly appeared on the bulletin board that classes were being suspended indefinitely. Even when I got together with my friends I hardly ever went drinking, but that day I went to a cheap drinking place alone. The situation made me think back over my college years. A great many thoughts came and went across my mind. It was a bitter accompaniment to my drinking. Chewing over this bitter fare I kept drinking steadily. No matter how much I drank I wasn't getting drunk.

While I was sitting there a bunch of college students came crowding into the place making a racket. I could see at a glance by their tanned skin and solid build that they were varsity athletes. After they sat down they kept talking raucously about athletic scouting. They were getting more excited as they talked about the price paid these days for players in each sport, or about how they say so-and-so went to some college because of a talent scout, and how another guy was going to go to some other college but the whole business was really rigged and he didn't make it. I took my cup and threw the contents in their direction.

You say you think that was daring? It was. It was just that I didn't have the constitution to put that kind of daring into practice naturally. When I threw the drink, all the faces on the other side of the room turned and focused on me with ridicule. Next I picked up the wine kettle and threw it in the direction of those faces. When one of them got up and looked as if he was going to come near me, I lost consciousness from a powerful shock delivered to my chin.

I don't know how much time passed, but I found a stranger helping me up by the shoulders. There was no one to be seen and everything was quiet all around. I spat out a salty liquid that had collected in my mouth.

"Come on!" The man spoke in a rough voice. I followed after the fellow with my hand under my chin. But the pain didn't especially bother me. Instead I felt so relieved that it puzzled me. Here I was being taken to the police station. I flopped down on my knees.

The young man said abruptly, "You think you're so great just because you're a college student?" and he let me have it on the side of the face.

I saw stars glittering, and as I tried to stand on my shaky and twisted knees, I said, "Well, I didn't ask to be a college student."

Then I saw stars again as I heard, "Still worked up, are you, you son-of-a-bitch?"

That's when it happened. A black shadow appeared in front of my eyes while I was still seeing the dazzling light from being hit. There was a black shadow the size of the man who stood before me blocking the way. The black shadow began to grow behind the man, until it was the size of the wall, then it filled the whole room. I shut my eyes tightly.

Well then, now I'll tell you about what I did to apply the things that had taken definite form in my thinking, the things that had just been vaguely floating in the back of my mind up to that time. I'll tell you right now.

In the evening on the day I saw that ridiculous fight between the boy and the girl in the street, I decided that I would go out to the end of the street about the time I used to come home from work and walk back and forth there until the woman came down the street. Sure enough, she walked down the steep hill at the usual time. But that day I failed in my plan because the men were playing chess in front of the broker's office, and there were also other people walking in the street. The next day she had someone with her, so I failed again. The day after that, I'm not sure whether she went out early, or was sick, or had stayed out the day before and not come home, but anyway, I didn't see her.

On the fourth day I finally got my chance. I stood casually at the foot of the street and sized up the situation. Luckily there was no one at the broker's office, and I didn't spot anyone walking in the street. I acted relaxed so no one would notice anything unusual, and I waited for her to come by. There she came down the street, holding the side of her long Korean skirt in a perfectly natural way. That day she was wearing a Korean skirt and top, of a pale orange color. She was about ten paces away almost opposite the spot where I was waiting, when I saw a man come out of a side street nearby, and then a woman carrying a shopping basket appeared behind him. "Oh no, I've failed again today," I thought. But then I thought again, "How stupid not to do this just because someone might see me." And I came to the conclusion, "I'll accomplish just that much more if other people see me do it."

I was determined to carry out what I had to do. I stood squarely in front of the woman and looked straight at her. She looked flustered and stopped walking. Before she knew what had happened I found the ties on her blouse and yanked them. The straps on both sides popped loose and let go. The woman covered her breasts with her hands. A look of utter astonishment came into her eyes, the natural rosy color blanched from the face which had so little make-up on it, and her mouth fell half open.

Without giving a moment's leeway, I grabbed the top of her skirt inside the open blouse and pulled hard. The tie holding up her slip snapped, the belt of her skirt slid down, exposing her full naked breasts. The woman gave a short scream.

When I saw her pretty face contorted into this strange ugliness, I turned away and began to run. I didn't know how I could run or where I would go, I just ran as hard as I could. It was a long while before I realized that I was running down a street quite far away from my neighborhood. I pushed people aside and kept right on running. I ran for a long time, until I was out of breath and simply couldn't run any more.

I found myself in front of a large corner store window. There was a mannequin standing inside, and also some legs propped upside down. There were stockings on the legs, a brassiere around the firmly protruding breasts of the mannequin, and gloves on some hands that were separated at the wrists.

Those hands with the black gloves were beckoning me to come. I went over close. My face was mirrored right between the stockings and the brassiere. That face! I rammed that face with my head. At the sharp sound of the shattering glass I felt my face relaxing. No, not just my face. My whole body, my whole self, began to feel relieved.

You say the scar on my forehead is going to last a long time? What difference does that make? After all, I *am* dead, you know. Not someone who's going to die later, I mean, but someone who's already dead. I died last night, or to be precise, I've been dead since three this morning. Just before then the room was light enough for me to see the wristwatch by my pillow. It read just a little before three o'clock. I checked it, though, and it was still going. Just the same, somehow I felt something was wrong with the watch.

I put on my slippers and decided to go down to the nurses' station. The slippers would not stay on because the soles of my feet were sweating. That made me aware that not just the soles of my feet, but my whole body was covered with cold sweat. In my sleep I had broken out in a cold sweat, struggling to keep my body from being dragged down by someone who was pulling from below. The thought then occurred to me that it was the same black figure who was trying to drag down my body. But there wasn't a sign of him anywhere. I left the room and went to the nurses' station. A nurse dressed in disturbing white was writing something on a sheet of paper. I asked the nurse what the time was. Without raising her head she pointed with the ballpoint pen in her hand to the wall behind her. A big round clock was on the wall. Sure enough, that clock also said three o'clock.

I was about to turn back, but stopped and told the nurse that my wound was bothering me and I couldn't sleep. I asked for something to take. I was frightened at the prospect of having to be awake until morning. It wasn't until then that the nurse finally raised her head and looked directly at me. I explained to her that I hadn't been able to sleep a wink yet. After a long wait, and with no expression on her face, the nurse took a white pill out of a bottle. It wasn't until I got back to my room that I discovered why it was so light there. There was a streetlight outside the window. After hesitating for a while over whether I should take the sedative or not, finally I just gulped it down, shook off the slick, moist slippers and got into bed.

It occurred to me that I would like just once to meet up with that black thief with my mind clear.

I seem to have fallen asleep for a moment without knowing it while I was waiting for the black figure to appear. But no, that's not right. I'm sure I was still wide awake. Someone began to pull me down toward the bottom of the bed. I could tell without looking that it had to be that black visitor. It was strange, though, I wasn't the least bit afraid.

As I was pulled down I gave in and didn't resist. After some time had passed I found myself in a space filled with darkness. When I examined it closely, there I was inside a grave. All four sides, top and bottom were completely enclosed in pitch darkness without a crack anywhere.

Then it came to me. That I had died. It all seemed so perfectly natural. It was sufficient to be in a peaceful state of death. Anyway the only reason I left the grave for a little while was so that I could talk with you. Now I have to go back.

When will I come out again? Well, I can't say. What's the date today, anyway? You say it's April 16th? And the year? So its April 16th, 1974? The 6's and the 9's are all mixed up again. If you straighten them out, it comes out April 19th, 1674. Do you understand? I'm thinking about coming out then, sometime in the real 1900's, not the 1600's mistakenly made over into 1900's. Then I'll make up all the time that was confiscated from me.

*Translated by Edward Poitras*

# Winter Forsythias

Sang-ch'ŏl smoked one cigarette after another outside the operating room. His sister-in-law Yŏng-i's surgery had taken so long – five and a half anxious hours. When the operation finally ended at six-thirty that evening, night had gathered over the late October day.

According to Yun, a resident in neurosurgery and a high school classmate of Sang-ch'ŏl's, they had cut away a growth the size of a small egg from the back of her brain. They were not yet sure if it was malignant.

Sang-ch'ŏl was led by Yun through a door marked "No Admittance" and into a recovery room. Yun had advised him not to let her mother and sister see Yŏng-i, and Sang-ch'ŏl had agreed. He was glad he had done so.

She was an appalling sight. Her head was completely swathed in a bandage, her eyes shielded from the light by cotton gauze. Her face was swollen and an oxygen tube had been inserted in her nose. She resembled neither Yŏng-i nor any other living person. They had placed her on her stomach for the operation, Yun explained, and thus the swelling.

When Yŏng-i was diagnosed as having a brain tumor, her mother had visited Sang-ch'ŏl to discuss whether or not to have surgery. Sang-ch'ŏl realized that Yŏng-i's father had passed away some years ago and her only brother was still in middle school. Yŏng-i's mother thus had no one but Sang-ch'ŏl to consult. Even so, Sang-ch'ŏl could not make a quick decision for her. He knew Korean medicine was such that seventy to eighty percent of those undergoing brain surgery died on the operating table or shortly thereafter. Twenty to thirty percent became hemiplegic or quadriplegic, and no one recovered completely. In the end they decided to have the surgery, because Yŏng-i herself, unable to endure the agonizing pain in her head, requested it in spite of the prospect of death.

Early the previous spring, at the beginning of her second year in high school, Yŏng-i had begun complaining that her head sometimes felt like it would explode when she got up after having lain down. They had brought her here to the university hospital, but the cause could not be found. She soothed the pain with analgesics and it lessened a bit over the summer, but with autumn it gradually intensified to the point where no medicine could alleviate it. In time she felt as if her brain were being seared by a hot iron. Sang-ch'ŏl could understand how Yŏng-i herself would want an operation, dangerous though it was.

It took five days for Yŏng-i to open her eyes, but she did not recognize anyone. Nor could she move or hear, much less speak.

Even patients whose condition was quite grave generally had to be moved to a ward two or three days after surgery, but Yŏng-i was able to remain in the recovery room for a week, thanks to Yun. During that time her condition neither improved nor deteriorated.

Meanwhile, the growth cut from her brain proved to be malignant. That meant Yŏng-i probably wouldn't last six months. This news demoralized the family, who, until now, had not given up hope. Sang-ch'ŏl's mother-in-law was hardest hit. She lost control of herself and appeared ready to collapse right in the hospital corridor.

Even after Yŏng-i was moved to a room of her own, her condition remained just the same. In any event, the family had to make the most of her life for as long as she lasted. They needed a professional who would look after her. And so they hired a nurse's aide.

The woman, introduced to them by someone at the hospital, looked a little over forty. She was rather short, but her sturdy frame and round face appeared healthy. That was a plus, agreed the family, but the drooping corners of her mouth and her fleshy upper eyelids somehow gave them the impression that she lacked warmth and attentiveness, that she was easily rubbed the wrong way. They doubted such a woman could attend to the every need of a patient entirely unable to make herself understood. Apart from turning Yŏng-i over every two hours to prevent abscesses and calluses on her back, there was the question of whether she could follow Yŏng-i's meal program. She was to feed Yŏng-i through a rubber tube in her nose connected with an I-V bottle containing first of all a mixture of milk, eggs, and rice gruel. Two hours later it was vegetable-beef broth, followed in another two hours by fruit juice. She was to do this three times a day, skipping only the night-time hours when Yŏng-i was asleep. Needless to say, she had to be punctual at each of these mealtimes, but she also had to regulate the thickness and temperature of the foods. The family worried whether the woman could carry out such duties.

And then there was a disquieting rumor about the woman. Until fairly recently she had performed various chores in the operating rooms and recovery ward in the university hospital, but then, so the story went, she was discharged because of a terrible blunder. A nurse in one of the recovery rooms had asked the woman to keep an eye on an intensive-care patient while she went to the toilet. When she returned, she found that the oxygen tube had slipped out of the patient's nose, and he had died. This story could only strengthen the family's fears that the woman was not suitable as a nurse's aide.

Sang-ch'ŏl's mother-in-law and wife seemed to agree with him on this. At the moment, though, there was no alternative. This was not a time to be selective; indeed, two registered nurse's aides from the university's department of nursing had been considered, but after seeing Yŏng-i's condition they had left, shaking their heads. Instead, the family had to be content with anybody willing to take care of the girl. They had no choice but to hire the woman temporarily until someone better could be found.

The family had a "No Visitors" sign posted on the door of Yŏng-i's room, and barred entry to everyone. Even Yŏng-i's home room teacher and school friends were always having to be turned away. The family did not worry that Yŏng-i would be traumatized by the looks of teachers or whomever, for she had lost all awareness. They just did not want anyone else to see the horrible condition she was in. They were afraid of gossip, so they explained to the woman in no uncertain terms that only family members were to be let into the room.

The swelling in Yŏng-i's face subsided before long, but she could not see, though she opened her eyes and rotated her eyeballs this way and that. Following her gaze and trying to make eye contact was indescribably frustrating and ultimately useless. Sang-ch'ŏl's mother-in-law and wife occasionally put their mouths right to her ear to call her name, and soon tears were trickling down their cheeks.

Her eyeballs and mouth were the only part of her that moved. Once in a while she opened her mouth in something like a yawn, and sometimes she seemed to smack her lips. Not a finger, a toe, or anything else moved even an inch. She was nothing but a lump of meat whose breathing had yet to stop.

But there were times when Yŏng-i showed faint signs of life. She occasionally looked pained when she was turned over or when her limbs were massaged and flexed by the hospital masseur so that joints and muscles would not stiffen. Even then, she made not a sound but merely grimaced. To be sure, ascertaining that Yŏng-i was alive through these pathetic contortions of her face was a sad and frustrating business, but the family felt grateful even for these expressions of pain. Besides, the doctor's statement that it could take three months or so for a patient to regain consciousness, depending on the case, gave them a ray of hope.

Facing the southeast, the room never seemed dim; nevertheless, the family brought a large indigo glass vase and kept it filled with fresh flowers to lessen the profound gloom that lingered there.

The New Year passed without the family's finding another nurse's aide. Yŏng-i's consciousness remained locked in darkness.

Through Yun's mediation, Yŏng-i's private room cost the family no more than a bed in a ward. No more did the family try to make eye contact with Yŏng-i. No more did they cry after calling her name.

To their surprise, though, the family found the woman's attention to Yŏng-i extraordinary, and it seemed more with each passing day. Perhaps their failure to find another aide was rather fortunate after all. Sang-ch'ŏl, for his part, regretted his initial, hasty judgment of the woman, but of course this regret did leave an unpleasant aftertaste.

The woman's silent care was not simply a duty she performed as an employee; rather, she had yielded herself up to Yŏng-i.

Some time earlier Yŏng-i had exchanged night with day. She now slept during the day and was awake at night. Although it was impossible for the woman to follow Yŏng-i in treating day as night and even though the woman sometimes fell asleep during the night, she never once neglected turning Yŏng-i over or feeding her. Even the doctors and nurses were amazed at this.

And then there was Yŏng-i's physical therapy: the woman would massage her when the hospital masseur was too busy. At such times Yŏng-i seemed to hurt less. After the change in Yŏng-i's sleeping schedule, more-over, the woman massaged her as the occasion demanded, regardless of the hour. Eventually the masseur became unnecessary.

Apart from that, the woman quickly perceived

every hint that Yŏng-i was cold or warm and reacted accordingly. Even before the goosebumps sprouted on Yŏng-i's face the woman would be tucking the quilt snug under her chin and adding a sweater or something on top. Even before the fever rose on her face the woman would be pulling back the quilt and placing her arms outside it.

Nor did the woman forget for even a day to moisten some gauze, always with lukewarm water, and wipe the patient's face, or to clean out her mouth with surgical cotton.

Winter passed in this fashion, and when spring arrived, the family discovered, to their disbelief, that a subtle bond had formed between the two.

Close to five months had elapsed since the operation. Yŏng-i was still comatose, so she urinated and defecated at any hour. Once the woman gave her a slap on the bottom after she wet a brand-new diaper. Tears ran down Yŏng-i's cheeks, as if she regretted having done this and was upset by the spanking.

Another time, while a nurse was taking her pulse, Yŏng-i bit her tongue after yawning. In no time she was bleeding, but she clenched her teeth so firmly that the nurse could not begin to open her mouth. The woman approached and stroked Yŏng-i's jaw while reasoning with her, "My sweet, don't do that. Open your mouth just a little. Come on now, hmm?" Only then, to everyone's amazement, did Yŏng-i relent.

One day Sang-ch'ŏl dropped by the hospital. He had been busy with work and this was his first visit for a while. He hesitated as he entered Yŏng-i's room. The linoleum floor was now immaculate, and he was afraid to step onto it without removing his shoes.

The woman was alone with Yŏng-i. The woman's face, which he had not seen for some time, looked abnormally haggard. The corners of her mouth drooped lower, and her fleshy upper eyelids had swollen so as to cover her eyes. It was the appearance of one who had suddenly aged several years. Accepting the chair she silently offered him, Sang-ch'ŏl said, "We appreciate all you've been doing." Her response was simple: "It's nothing."

The woman removed Yŏng-i's woolen hat to reveal her hair. It had been closely cropped before the operation, but was now like the tousled hair of a tomboy. Although it was daytime, Yŏng-i was awake. When Sang-ch'ŏl asked whether Yŏng-i's sleeping schedule was back to normal, the woman hesitated for a moment, then said, "The dear thing's probably sorry I can't sleep at night."

Sang-ch'ŏl could not take his eyes off Yŏng-i's face for some time. Though lacking its former fullness and apple-red cheeks, it had given bloom to a lovely complexion. The furrows carved between her eyebrows, a sign of her suffering before the operation, had been smoothed away. The doctors had said she probably wouldn't last six months if the growth was malignant, yet in no way did her face look like the face of one confronting death.

Just then Sang-ch'ŏl heard the woman's voice behind him: "Sweetie, do you want to go potty?" It was the unnaturally high voice of an adult talking to a small child. He could not believe it was really her voice. Sang-ch'ŏl studied Yŏng-i's expression. There was not the slightest change; she merely cast a vacant stare into nothingness. The woman said, "Sweetie, you can wait a little bit, hmm?" Sang-ch'ŏl looked back at the woman, struck by the unvarying coaxing tone. The woman spread out a piece of newspaper in readiness for a bowel movement, and her eyes came to rest on Yŏng-i's face. Sang-ch'ŏl's heart glowed when he saw the expression that broke through the woman's swollen eyelids. She was clearly reading something in Yŏng-i's blank face. He realized that he ought to leave at once.

On the way out he stopped at Yun's office. "She looks quite good. What do you think?"

Yun tilted his head and said, "Well . . . ," then continued with a smile: "Even if she stays like that, there's no telling when there might be a sudden change. It's a condition that doesn't allow for predictions."

Under such circumstances, the family's visits gradually became more sporadic. They came to the hospital no more than once every ten or fifteen days, to pay for Yŏng-i's food or the woman's services. Not only did they trust the woman and feel safe with her, but they were also quite worn out.

The flowers in the vase, if any, were always withered. The vase looked hollow and bigger than before.

The woman's face looked worse and worse, to the point where her naturally round features had become shriveled and unsightly. On the other hand, Yŏng-i passed the summer with no noticeable abscesses and no heat rashes. There was only a slightly softened hipbone, which healed. At the same time, her complexion took on a pearly bloom that was even more lovely than before. Her hair had grown quite long enough to be pinned up here and there.

The doctors had said Yŏng-i probably wouldn't last six months because of the malignancy, but here it was ten months later. With summer almost over, one afternoon Sang-ch'ŏl's wife called him at work. The hospital had notified her that Yŏng-i was in a critical condition. So we've reached the inevitable, thought Sang-ch'ŏl.

Sang-ch'ŏl found Yun, Yŏng-i's doctor, and some nurses providing emergency treatment, giving Yŏng-i a blood transfusion and oxygen. His mother-in-law and wife were standing behind them, their faces cloaked in handkerchiefs that muffled their sobbing.

Yŏng-i's breath was rushing out of her open mouth, and her round, gaping eyes were fixed on one spot as if she were about to pass on. It seemed an agonizing final hour.

Hearing a discordant sound amid the weeping of his mother-in-law and wife, Sang-ch'ŏl looked back. There in a corner, beside the cooking utensils, the woman was squatting with her face buried in her arms atop her raised knees. She seemed so small.

It was not so much crying as a moaning sob that she was trying to stifle. It was like a moan that leaked out in spite of her attempts to suppress all her surging emotions. This sound alone, trailing from the woman, kept penetrating Sang-ch'ŏl's ears.

Yŏng-i surprised everyone that day by surviving. Her eyes widened for a while, and after gasping as if she would breathe her last at any minute, she broke out in a heavy sweat, then drifted off to sleep.

Sang-ch'ŏl had become tangled in a strange thought: beyond any doubt Yŏng-i had fallen asleep while listening to the woman's moaning sobs. He wanted to believe this, even before reckoning whether it was possible or not.

The woman continued to sob for a while even after the doctors and nurses had left and Sang-ch'ŏl's mother-in-law and wife had stopped crying.

The day Yŏng-i passed away, some three months later, sleet was flying in every direction. It had been thirteen and a half months since the operation.

Sang-ch'ŏl hurried to the hospital with his wife, who had taken a taxi to his office and picked him up. The hospital had informed her of Yŏng-i's death and urged them to come at once.

Sang-ch'ŏl's mother-in-law arrived about the same time. She lived far from the hospital and might have had trouble catching a taxi, Sang-ch'ŏl thought. The two women hugged each other and burst into tears.

Sang-ch'ŏl asked what had happened. The woman looked down and did not answer. Her eyelids seemed heavier than before.

As Sang-ch'ŏl lifted his gaze from the silent woman, the forsythias in the vase on the nightstand caught his eye. There was a scattering of blossoms on the straggly sprigs sticking out from the vase. The woman had cut them somewhere and put them there before they bloomed. Perhaps because the flowers had bloomed out of season, at a time of year when sleet was falling, their distinctive vivid yellow seemed to be reflected in everything, even the white bed sheet that covered the corpse.

Sang-ch'ŏl was about to ask the woman again what had happened, when it occurred to him that these flowers, and not the woman, were telling him there was nothing to say.

Sang-ch'ŏl decided to visit Yun. From the beginning of their conversation Yun lacked his usual smile. "When I went in," Yun said, "she'd already been dead for a while." He was implying that it was not the hospital's fault that the family had not been notified of Yŏng-i's imminent death. "In other words, the woman didn't call a nurse until after she had died," Yun continued. "I ran to the room when I got the news, and the woman had already closed the patient's eyes and put cotton balls in her nostrils."

Recalling the woman's grief three months before, Sang-ch'ŏl asked, "So she was the only one with her at the end?"

"Yes." After a pause, Yun added, "This time, she was standing next to the bed and there wasn't much crying – not like last time anyway."

Even when Sang-ch'ŏl's mother-in-law and wife burst into tears, the woman had not wept. Did this mean she had finished her crying before anybody came? Sang-ch'ŏl wondered.

"Do you think she was suffering at the end?" Sang-ch'ŏl asked, remembering Yŏng-i's previous agony.

"I really couldn't say, since I wasn't there . . . I remember this, though. The nurse told me that since the last time, the woman was always reasoning with her, 'Sweetie, even if you're going to die, do it nicely. Do it nicely, hmm?' You know, I'm not sure if it was that or something else, but her face was clean and she looked like someone in a deep sleep, completely at peace with herself. Her hair had just been washed, and you could see it had been nicely combed . . . People with brain damage are usually vomiting at the end – it's not very peaceful."

Sang-ch'ŏl lit a cigarette, then offered one to Yun.

Yun declined, explaining that he had just finished one, then continued. "It wasn't a sickroom. It was a room where two people were living together. Lately, believe it or not, doctors, nurses, and anyone else who visited that room had to take off their shoes. And if either of them caught a cold or something, then the other one usually would too. I don't think you can find that kind of relationship even between parents and their children. Those two understood each other more than we'll ever know. The woman probably knew when Yŏng-i would die, too. I'd have to say she didn't inform us even though she knew it was coming."

Sang-ch'ŏl had nothing more to say or hear. The woman's utterly devoted care seemed to have over-turned a medical diagnosis and prolonged Yŏng-i's life. And as long as Yŏng-i could not return to normal, Sang-ch'ŏl had thought, it was better that she pass on while in a coma.

When it came time to wash and shroud the body, the family let the woman dress it as she wished.

After the body was transferred to the mortuary, Sang-ch'ŏl's wife went to the hospital gift shop to buy candles. Upon her return she hurriedly informed Sang-ch'ŏl, "I just heard she quit her job as a nurse's aide. She took her name off the register and left."

Sang-ch'ŏl looked out of the window. He had expected this.

It was cloudless and mild for the funeral two days later. The woman's familiar figure was absent then too.

*Translated by Bruce and Ju-chan Fulton*

# Folding the Umbrella

Old Mr Hŏ couldn't forget about the black mollie. It kept running through his mind that there was no difference between the fish and the image he had of Hye-gyŏng.

Hŏ entered the flower shop and slowly turned his gaze from one flower to the next. He was unable to decide whether to buy a potted plant or a bouquet, but there was no need to hurry. He still had plenty of time.

Several days after Hye-gyŏng became engaged she told him about a dream she had had. She was at the wedding hall, and when it came her turn to go in following the entrance of the groom, she casually glanced up at the mirror and was startled: her wedding dress was black.

As he had listened to Hye-gyŏng talk about her dream, the black mollies immediately came to mind. The color of the tropical fish resembled soft black velvet.

"Anyway, it looks like my marriage is going to be unlucky."

"Nonsense, if you see something bad in a dream, it's actually a good sign."

But in fact, he was thinking that the black mollie

truly was a lonely and unfortunate creature.

Last spring he had bought two pair of black mollies about a month after they were born. Although he had raised many species of tropical fish, this was the first time he had handled black mollies.

It was also the first time he had dealt with such a difficult fish to raise. Before they were fully grown he lost three and was barely able to save the last one, a female. Although it usually requires an expert to distinguish the sex of goldfish or tropical fish when they are young, as they mature their shapes become different enough for anyone to be able to tell the male and female apart. The male's figure was long and slender, while the female's protruding belly gave it a roundish shape. A long time had already passed since the lone surviving black mollie had revealed itself to be a female.

As the fish matured and its mating season approached, its bosom, like that of a woman, had swelled, and its sleek black velvety skin had taken on a gloss.

In order to find a mate for the black mollie, Hŏ first went to the store where he had purchased it. Then he scoured every last establishment that specialized in fish. Still, his search proved in vain.

The owner of a shop in Namyŏng-dong called "The Aquarium" told Hŏ that he was sold out of black mollies at present, but he was able to notify Hŏ of the whereabouts of the man who had bought them. Hŏ went to visit this man, but he said that he, too, had been unsuccessful and that all his black mollies had died.

The proprietor of one fish store, in mentioning that

he had heard of a man in Pusan who was raising black mollies, commented that this fish preferred water that was alkaline. Since Seoul's water appeared to be on the acidic side, he went on, Seoul and black mollies were incompatible. Still, it wasn't as if Hŏ could just run off to Pusan, so from that time on he had been adding bicarbonate of soda to the water and paying particular attention to controlling the temperature.

Nevertheless, his belief that disaster would befall the lonely fish before he could find a mate for it secretly continued to grow stronger.

Finally Hŏ wound up deciding on the bouquet. Even though cut flowers would wither, it seemed better to celebrate her marriage this way than to send a potted plant that would require trouble.

He had them fashion a bouquet out of red carnations only. After informing them of the wedding hall and the time, he paid for the flowers and requested that they be delivered.

Music had been the medium through which he had come to know Hye-gyŏng.

It was after he had been forced to retire as a pianist. Certainly he was getting on in years, but one day while he was absorbed in practicing for a concert to commemorate his sixtieth birthday, his left arm had become paralyzed unexpectedly. Although the disease was not fatal, the use of his arm could not be fully restored.

When he could no longer play the keyboard himself, his opportunities to listen to others' performances naturally increased, and he had to be content with that. From time to time he used to stop in and buy newly-released records at the music store where Hye-gyŏng worked.

Hye-gyŏng had musical talent beyond the training required of a mere employee at a music store. She seemed to have a particular affinity for the piano. Her figure was well-proportioned all around, but her long fingers were perfectly suited for the piano. It was a pity her family circumstances prevented her from studying the piano intensively.

As time went on, he would drop by Hye-gyŏng's store to rest, even when he wasn't buying records.

Hŏ left the florist's and started his meandering journey. His shadow stretched off somewhat before him to the right.

As if looking at his reflection in the sunlight, he lifted both hands and examined their backs. Age spots dotted his wrinkled skin. More of these discolorations lay on his left hand than his right.

Sometimes when Hye-gyŏng could leave the shop, the two of them would stroll about and she would inevitably grasp his left arm. As she did so, she would massage it casually with her hand. He understood why. She felt sorry for his paralyzed limb and wanted to do something for it. One time she even went so far as to say to Hŏ, "Isn't there a composer named Ravel? Maurice Ravel? Once a pianist he was friendly with had his right arm wounded in the war and couldn't use it, so Ravel wrote something called the 'Piano Concerto for the Left Hand,' didn't he? If I were a composer, I would have written you a 'Piano Concerto for the Right Hand.' "

"You've been lending me the hand I can't use, so you don't need to compose anything."

When they sat side by side in his house at the piano to play, she used to provide his left hand. At first there was no way they could keep together and they would have to play pieces over and over. Still he did not find it tedious. Little by little they learned to match rhythms. As he rested his left arm on her shoulder, he would reach the point of fantasizing that her left arm was his own and he would slip into a state of perfect selflessness.

Even though they were light melodies, on days when they played several pieces in this way, he somehow felt as though his home was complete. His children had already moved away and since his wife had died three years earlier, his household had been empty except for a maid.

Hŏ walked slowly. It wasn't as though he had wandered aimlessly, however, for he had arrived in front of a goldfish store. He entered and came out with some water fleas and feed worms.

"I hope nothing has happened to the black mollie," he thought.

Life is fleeting in general, but there is no creature whose existence is as ephemeral as a goldfish or tropical fish. Before an owner is aware that his pet is dying, it may already have lost its life, its head fixed in the sand at the bottom of the tank, or its body floating motionlessly on the surface belly up.

Three of his four black mollies had died and he could not know when the surviving fish would also meet its end. He simply had the notion that its death would differ greatly from that of the other fish. He believed that this black mollie, unable to overcome the loneliness pent up within it, would explode. It probably was nothing more than an absurd fantasy, but nevertheless that was how he imagined his fish would die.

Right about now Hye-gyŏng was probably in the bride's waiting room, waiting for the entrance of the groom, and she was probably looking at her own reflection in the mirror hanging on the wall. In her pure white wedding veil and her pure white gown, she was probably mulling over the black dress she had seen in her dream some time ago. Still, despite whatever feeling this memory imparted to her, it was clear that she was going to be married.

In that sense she was no longer the black mollie.

In raising tropical fish he had mated them several times. Among the various fish, the reproductive behavior of the blue gourami was a little unusual. First the male would spit out a bubbly foam on the water's surface, then coil itself around the female's pelvic region. A flawless, vigorous dance. Then the male would take the eggs laid by the female in its mouth one by one and insert them into the foam.

The reproductive act of the swordtail, which bore its young alive rather than lay eggs, was also somewhat strange.

When the female reached sexual maturity, its body became particularly beautiful and its scales became shinier. Hŏ placed the male, which he had previously separated off, in the female's tank. First the male pecked at the female's stomach, and then, reclining at approximately a forty-five degree angle, it grazed against the female's underbelly. Another vivid and delightful physical game.

He had known when he bought them that black

mollies also bore their young alive. He wondered what mating ritual these fish undertook.

Hŏ had not walked far from Hye-gyŏng's music store. He was on the street where she had told him about the dream she had shortly after her engagement. It was here as well that she had informed him of the wedding date.

That evening he had escorted her by taxi to her home in Kup'abal for the last time.

They had passed through Yŏngch'ŏng and when they reached Hongje-dong it became foggy. The mist fluctuated oddly, first being so thick as to impede their progress and then clearing soon after. In the heavy fog, the headlights of approaching cars would spread in circumference, so that the beams seemed to be emerging from deep water.

At the entrance to Kup'abal, Hye-gyŏng made a gesture as if to stop the taxi. Then she turned toward Hŏ.

"Let's go until we get to a place where the fog has lifted, Mr Hŏ."

Instead of answering, he merely nodded.

They had not gone far, however, before they escaped the fog completely. After driving a little while, Hye-gyŏng suggested they turn around. Hŏ wondered whether the fog had brought her insignificant dream back to life. As they returned, the fog, patches and all, quickly disappeared and the air kept on clearing, leaving only a haze behind.

The maid opened the front door.

"Your eldest just left a little while ago, Mr Hŏ."

His sons would both stop in once or twice a month

to see how their father was doing.

"He said he would come here tomorrow for breakfast, sir."

He asked whether there was some special occasion for his grandchildren.

"Isn't tomorrow your birthday, sir?"

Oh, that's right, he thought. Hŏ habitually forgot his own birthday.

So, tomorrow we'll all gather at my youngest son's, thought Hŏ, and there the older will again suggest that I come live with him in order to save face. He'll say it tears at his heart to leave an old man by himself. But I'll tell him not to worry and to just let me stay like this.

After going to his room and changing into his house clothes, he distributed the water fleas and worms, which he had been holding in a plastic bag, among the fish tanks.

He was bringing the black mollie up in a separate aquarium. He watched it peck at its food.

The black mollie was now even glossier and had a more velvety texture. As the fish darted cheerfully about, it gradually became magnified before his eyes. The entire tank grew black.

Without his realizing it, Hŏ's hand descended into the fish tank. It took a little time. At last he applied pressure to the slippery object within his grasp.

*Translated by Stephen Epstein*

# For Dear Life

Muzzles glared ominously over the barricades thrown up in front of the presidential mansion. But the students, locked in columns resembling so many football formations, had nothing to fear. Their arms were linked into a determined mass in which one stood for all and all for one. Jun-o was one of the links. The columns started moving. They had one more barrier to crush; they felt confident they could do it. One more thrust was all they needed. The resolute mass kept forging ahead. Then, all of a sudden things took an evil turn. No sooner had the muzzles opened up on them than Jun-o found himself dislodged from his column, for his comrade to the left had fallen forward, releasing his grip on Jun-o. Jerking his arm loose from his comrade on the right, Jun-o groped his way out of the crowd.

Jun-o felt as though someone were chasing him, as though a rifle were being aimed to lodge a hot bullet in his back. Turning down an alley, he hid in the first house he could barge into. Crouching in the corner of the living room, he tried to collect himself but could not control his trembling. Nevertheless, he felt relieved and gratified that, after all, he had not been shot down. He decided he would now shut himself up in his boarding house until the situation grew quieter.

Later that day, nevertheless, Jun-o was shot in the leg.

He had remained in his refuge for a while even after peace had been restored in the neighborhood. Then, carefully tracing his way through narrow alleys, he made it all the way to the Seoul Railroad Station. Just as he was about to cross over T'oegyero Street, he heard shots from behind. Now he had no time to hide. A heavy slug pierced his right leg and he fell forward. People were running in all directions.

The shooting stopped and the area became quiet. Jun-o tried to rise only to collapse again. He ran a groping hand down his numb right leg and touched something sticky. Scared and trembling all over, he simply did not dare to try to rise again.

Now someone was running toward him – it was a woman. The shooting resumed but the woman did not stop.

Silently, the woman pulled Jun-o up with her shoulder under his arm. The shots cracked in the dark and pellets pinged off the ground near them. The shots were fired from an elevated position.

After leaving Jun-o at a nearby hospital, the woman did not show up again. She was a complete stranger to him but somehow he felt he would recognize her if he saw her again.

The day he left hospital he set out to look for the woman after sending his sister (who had come up from Pusan to look after him) back to his boarding house. His legs were still stiff and so he walked slowly, probing his memory as he went. He turned into an alley between Severance Hospital and South Gate. He had not noticed it before, but there were now burned-out coal briquets on the rugged back alley lined by uneven rows of houses. The wine shops and soup stalls on either side reeked of steamy pork and fish entrails. Jun-o hated the smell and held his breath as he walked on.

Nearly all the shops and houses were flimsy shacks. At the corner of one shack a man stood urinating. A shrill female voice poured abuse at him from inside the shack, but the man kept on quite oblivious. Only her voice came from inside the room; the woman did not look out at the entrance.

Jun-o stepped over to one of the little shacks. It looked like the house in front of which the woman had paused, as if to enter, on their way to the hospital. Instead of entering she had merely torn a strip of cloth off the hem of her skirt in order to bind his wounded leg and had dragged him on to the hospital with his arm wrapped around her shoulder. She had acted calmly and coolly then. But what about now? Jun-o wondered.

Taking another look at the shack to make sure it was the right place, Jun-o called for the mistress of the house. There was no answer. He called again, a little louder, but still no response. He cautiously pulled at the door only to find that it was locked from the inside. Maybe there is another door through which the occupants pass.

He turned to face the street vendor at an open stall a few steps away. She must have been watching him, for she was shaking her tanned face at him. When

Jun-o looked at her inquiringly, she suggested that he come back after dark. This could only mean the mistress of the house was not in. He had no choice but to leave.

While lying on his hospital bed, Jun-o would turn his face away whenever he saw newspaper headlines extolling "The Heroes of the April Revolution" or "The Young Lions". He would keep his eyes closed when visitors came to comfort the wounded. He felt the blood rush to his face and his heart pounded whenever he recalled the event. In such excitement a figure always loomed up in his mind – a woman running toward him braving all those bullets. The fragile shoulder he had held on to. He still felt the touch of her shoulder blades in his palms. "Who are you?" Jun-o had asked her. Barely supporting his weight, she had silently looked at Jun-o. Although her face was covered with beads of perspiration, it had a composed look. He now visualized his own face superimposed on hers – the face of a shivering deserter. *I will never amount to anything unless I am part of an organized body. I flee danger, yet wish that this woman would hurry up and help me without considering her own safety. At least I should have grabbed the shoulder of the student next to the one who had been shot down in front of the presidential mansion. I should have marched on. I am a coward, a craven coward.*

Jun-o often dreamed that he was being squeezed under a devilish weight. He could not recall whether it was early dawn or early evening, but he had found himself in the middle of a dark street. Scraps of paper fluttered in the wind. He imagined that he should collect them. Incapable of voluntary movement, the scraps of paper, as it were, symbolized himself. Although he tried with all his power to pick them up, he was unable to do so because his legs would not move the way he wanted them to.

This feeling of impotence nagged him even while he was awake. He lost confidence in himself and in everything else.

The woman's house was unlit when he visited there again after dark. Apparently the people of the house had not yet returned. He went over to speak to the street vendor whose stall was lit by a candle. She advised him to wait a while. He wanted to repay her kindness by buying something from her, but there was nothing among her wares he really needed. So he bought a packet of cigarettes even though he did not smoke, and asked her if the mistress of the house always returned late. Her answer was simply that he would have to wait just a little while.

A few women, their faces powdered white, walked past him quietly. A boy, who must have been under ten years old, ran out to the woman's stall to buy a bottle of *soju* and a dried cuttlefish and disappeared again with his purchases into the dark of the alley.

A little later the street vendor motioned him with her head to look at the ray of light leaking through a crack in the paper door of the house. The door soon opened and a man carried his shoes outside, put them on, and strolled off toward T'oegyero Street. From the very outset Jun-o suspected the foul trade going on in this alley. And her house was no exception.

Nevertheless, Jun-o could not shake off his wistfulness. He felt he should leave but something held him back. The door opened again and a woman stepped out carrying her rubber shoes in one hand and buttoning her blouse with the other. With her back to the light, it was impossible to see who she was. Jun-o stepped over to her, his heart throbbing. The woman cast a suspicious glance at him. Now Jun-o knew it was the woman he had been looking for.

A little hesitant, Jun-o said, "I left the hospital today."

The woman looked a little surprised but nevertheless identified the visitor in the dark. But she disappeared inside immediately. Jun-o groped around in the dark.

"Wait, I was going to thank you."

"Never mind the thanks."

"But I have something else to tell you, too."

"What is it you want to tell me? Come in anyway."

"No, not now. I've found out where you live and so I'll come back tomorrow. I hope you won't keep your door locked."

The woman remained silent.

As he trudged out of the alley he saw a woman bargaining with a drunken man.

The door was locked on the inside as before. Jun-o shook it with such force that the flimsy shack shuddered.

The street vendor feigned ignorance while passersby stole glances at him. Jun-o had not come here as one of her customers but he blushed, nevertheless.

It was some time before he heard someone opening the door from inside. The woman grimaced because of the glittering city lights as she greeted him. Her hair was dishevelled. She stepped aside to make way for him to enter. She eyed the shoes he had taken off outside, and so he picked them up and carried them inside.

In the dark room the bedding had been pushed aside haphazardly. She sat next to the bedding, facing Jun-o, and lit a cigarette. She appeared eager to listen to him. Her face was lean and her skin coarse.

Unable to start talking immediately, Jun-o diverted his attention to the dressing table in the corner. Yellowish patches were reflected in the mirror from the light filtering through cracks in the wooden planking of the wall pasted over with old newspapers.

"Is your wound all healed up now?" the woman spoke first.

"Yes."

"I'm happy to hear it."

"I could have died if I'd been left there alone."

But what he really wanted to say was something else. With his eyes glued on the yellowish patches on the mirror, he continued, "I'd like to know what made you brave all those bullets to . . ."

The woman replied in a chilly yet placid voice, "Well, maybe I wanted to be shot down myself."

"Why? Are you tired of life?"

"Let's not get involved in each other's private lives. That day was that day and everything is over now."

Jun-o wanted to know what exactly she meant by "maybe I wanted to be shot down myself."

He called on her a few more times on his way home from the university when his lectures ended early.

Each time, however, he had to leave disappointed.

She merely kept chainsmoking, filling her room with smoke, while he tried to reach her mind. So he would leave without getting any closer to the innermost recesses of her heart. There was no halfway point where they could meet.

But one day he found her drunk. She was lying on her mattress, wearing a faraway, abstracted look.

"Those bastards don't even know common decency! Why, people turn their faces away even when dogs do it. Who do those bastards think they are? Are they going to feed us?" she was saying to herself.

With a start she pulled on her clothes and limped out of the room. Jun-o had no choice but to sit and wait.

Presently she returned with a tray containing two bowls of *sŏnji* soup. One bowl had spilled over a little as she limped in. Offering one bowl to Jun-o, she began eating her soup, bluish veins bulging at her temple as she ate.

Although he had seen it before, this was Jun-o's first opportunity to taste such soup. It smelled fishy and its taste was nauseating. He literally had to struggle with the few spoonfuls he tried.

"Maybe this kind of food doesn't suit your taste because you've grown up in a rich family. Why don't you go home and have some poached eggs?" she said, casting a relaxed but sour look at Jun-o.

Jun-o did not know whether to take it seriously or as a joke; he merely stared at her.

"Why do you come here and just sit like that? You disturb my rest . . ."

She held the bowl in her hand and gulped down what was left in it.

"You don't need to keep coming here looking

stuck-up. Do you think I want to be your friend? I tell you, that day I went out early to find a customer after I'd gone without one for several days because of the demonstrations. And you were the first one I picked up. Only I didn't know you were so seriously wounded . . ."

Jun-o rushed out of the house, shivering. Shivering like the time he hid after running away from the march. Only this time it was his mind, not his body, that was trembling.

What had happened was completely alien to his life. Perhaps she was right when she told him they should not get involved in each other's private lives.

On the campus Jun-o tried to avoid the attention of his friends who regarded him as one of the wounded heroes of the April Revolution. *I am no hero of the Revolution nor anything else, I was simply shot in the leg trying to get away.* And he hated himself for not being able to tell the truth. But it was something which could not be helped. Whenever he went to the public bathhouse he would conceal his scar with a towel lest someone should question him about it.

One day, after he had stopped visiting the woman, Jun-o received a package from his parents in Pusan. It contained material for a woman's dress. He had asked them for it immediately after leaving hospital and now it had finally arrived. He hesitated for a while, but then he felt, after all, the gift must be presented to her.

One afternoon, when he was free from lectures, Jun-o set out from his boarding house carrying the package.

Walking down the alley toward her little shack, he heard the street vendor call him abruptly to stop. She waved her hand for him to come close to her and then whispered that the woman's husband had returned from prison.

Did she have a husband? Was she, then, doing it to make a living while her husband was in jail? Jun-o shuddered once again.

Of course he had nothing to worry about even if her husband should show up. At the same time there was no particular reason for him to stay around, either. Jun-o handed the package to the street vendor and, asking her to deliver it for him, turned to leave. He wondered if the couple in the house could enjoy their *sŏnji* soup together as if nothing had happened.

While waiting for the bus after stepping out of the alley, Jun-o found himself confronted by a heavily bearded man.

"I live in that house," the bearded man said. He was a lean man of average height wearing only shorts and a T-shirt. He looked well past thirty.

"I'm the husband of the woman who saved your life some time ago."

He did not stop to let Jun-o speak.

"Thanks for the gift. Now I have a favor to ask you. I wish you would help my wife while I'm away. I don't want you to help her for nothing. Just buy her flesh at the going rate from time to time. That'll help us a lot more than all those rallies and demonstrations. By the way, I understand my wife tore a piece of cloth from her skirt to tie up your wounded leg. Could you pay me for that now?"

Obediently Jun-o handed him all the money he had

with him. His hands were shaking and his heart was heavy. He felt crushing humiliation. He wanted to get away from it all as fast as he could.

A few days later Jun-o met the woman's husband again under unusual circumstances.

Jun-o was stepping out of the barbershop after a haircut when he heard someone shouting, "Thief!" Skillfully dodging an oncoming vehicle, a man was running across to his side of the street.

The runner was the woman's husband. He seemed to recognize Jun-o and stopped in front of him, flashing a smile. The smile almost concealed his eyes, which looked a little tired but bright in his jerky, bearded face.

A stout middle-aged man, who had been on his trail shouting "Thief!" behind the stream of traffic, finally managed to get across. Just as the stout man was about to step on the curb, the woman's husband who had been standing in front of Jun-o turned around and started running along a back street. Jun-o's heart was pounding. He felt he should have made a move to try and catch him. Perhaps the man had stopped in front of him, deliberately challenging him to make an arrest.

The next moment Jun-o swayed backward. The powerful grip of the middle-aged man held the scruff of his neck.

"You son-of-a-bitch: so, you're one of them? Well, let's go!" the middle-aged man shouted at Jun-o, glancing around to find a police box.

"Wait, you're making a mistake. I've got nothing to do with the whole thing."

"You bastard, I just saw you with my own eyes . . . Quit talking and follow me."

"But please take your hand off my neck."

A crowd gathered. With his neck in the grip of the middle-aged man, Jun-o was being dragged away.

"I said get your hand off my neck."

Jun-o's voice was not clear because his neck was in the man's grip and because his heart was trembling with rage.

The middle-aged man merely tightened his grip.

Jun-o knew words would do no good. The injustice of it stung him. He planted his feet firmly on the ground. Then he braced himself and started flailing with his fists. A punch landed squarely on the face of the middle-aged man who cried out and covered it with his hand. At this moment Jun-o gave him a kick in the shins and then ran for dear life, zigzagging through the crowd. For once he felt as though he had all the agility he needed.

*Translated by Song Yo-in*

# Blood

The boy had caught a honeybee. The bee had crawled inside a pumpkin flower, and he caught it by pinching together the ends of the petals. A nimble feat for a six-year-old.

He picked the pumpkin flower enclosing the honeybee and put it to his ear. The bee buzzed inside the flower. The child's mouth fell open wide, and wrinkles appeared in rows on his face, tanned golden by the sun.

The pumpkins had been planted in a small piece of open ground in front of his family's tent. Houses were to be built here sometime in the future, so garbage had been hauled from the city to make a landfill. This made the pumpkins bear well.

Once the boy had tried quite innocently to catch a bee in his hand. He sprang back in shock and burst out crying. Where did that little bee get such a dreadful thing? His mother pulled out the stinger from his hand and applied soybean paste, but it had smarted for a long time.

The boy learned from his mother to grasp the ends of the petals instead, but bees seldom came to this tent village. If by chance he happened to see one in a flower, it would fly away before he could catch it.

Every time this happened, the boy would gaze off into the endless sky where the bee had disappeared. He had thought a honeybee would never come again, but today, having caught one quite skillfully, he could not help but be overjoyed.

The boy wanted to show it to one of his friends, but the child he always played with next door had been sick for several days. Another friend's family had sold their tent and moved away. The new child who had moved in was a girl. He had not made friends with her yet.

As he was putting the buzzing flower bag to his ear, he heard from inside his family's tent the sound of ground squirrels scampering about in their cage bound with bush clover. They seemed to have eaten all their rations. The boy's mother had gone to the dump to pick rags, but he wished she would hurry back with food for the squirrels.

Thinking his father had said this morning that the squirrel buyer might come by, he walked between the tents and climbed the path behind them up the hill. He was barefoot, and the only thing he wore was a tattered shirt. His stomach bulged enormously, and his navel protruded even further through his torn shirt. Having lost their home in the flood the previous year, the boy's family had come to live in this tent village. Once here, the child could fill his empty stomach with all the pumpkin gruel he wanted, so he grew potbellied. When he walked, it was as if a huge belly were walking alone. His arms and legs were thin and gaunt by comparison.

At the end of the tent village was a sweet potato

patch that one of the refugees was cultivating. Bindweed flowers bloomed on the embankment around it. The boy felt a need to pee. Why did looking at these trumpet-shaped flowers make him have to pee? He wore no pants, so it was no trouble; he simply stood there to relieve himself. The yellow stream struck the flowers.

Just beyond the sweet potato patch, the boy's father was digging up large pieces of rock, preparing to plant autumn vegetables. The boy walked up to his father and held out the pumpkin flower.

"Papa, . . . a bee. I caught a bee."

The boy's father stopped his work and stared at the pumpkin flower. "That was some trick." Then, hobbling on his lame leg, he picked up a large rock to move it. "Hold it carefully while you're playing with it. And don't get stung again."

"I won't. I caught it the way Mama taught me to."

The boy climbed up the hillside path. He was not bored today even though he was alone. Over and over he put the pumpkin flower bag to his ear. When he could hear no sound, he shook the flower. Then the buzzing started again. No matter how much he thought about it, the boy could not get over his pride at having caught a honeybee.

Having reached a spot where stones stuck out of the ground ruggedly, the boy started to rub the sole of his foot on a rock. It was his habit when he came to this rough place. "I'm not going to break my leg like Papa did." He rubbed one foot for a while, then changed to the other.

Trees stood sparsely above this spot. There were

almost no pines, but other trees grew there, mostly brushwood, scrub oak, and overcup oak.

The boy walked up to the trees. The full leaves cast cool, luxuriant shade. The boy rummaged through the grass with his foot, feeling for acorns. They could hardly be plentiful. If he happened to find one, it was usually rotten. And the occasional sound ones were all black and hard as rocks. When he put one in his mouth it cracked and a bitter liquid seeped out. Still, it was better than nothing at all. As the boy put the bee to his ear again, he thought how wonderful it would be if acorns were candy.

The boy looked for acorns awhile. Then something darted out in front of him. It was a squirrel. The boy stiffened and watched. The squirrel climbed nimbly up one of the scrub oak trees. The boy held his breath as he caught the squirrel's movements. It went out on a branch about halfway up the tree, stopped there, then turned toward the boy, its tail curled up over its back.

I should hurry to tell Papa, thought the boy, but before he could turn to go, the squirrel scampered down the tree. The boy stiffened again, watching the animal's behavior. The squirrel did not rest on reaching the bottom of the tree, but ran off in the opposite direction. The boy found himself chasing after it in spite of himself – the skinny legs and potbelly tottered off. It was impossible for him to keep up with the squirrel. Still, he pursued it with all his might. The squirrel, in turn, came in and out of sight among the grass and bushes, and finally darted into a hole under a tree stump. The boy stopped and scrutinized the hole, then turned and began to hurry down the hill. "The squirrel went in a hole! The squirrel went in a hole!"

The boy emerged from the shade of the trees into the blazing sun. He passed the spot where the rugged stones lay in the ground.

His father should have been working in the field, but the boy could not see him. He rushed on. Just as he was about to pass the sweet potato patch, the pumpkin flower he had been holding in his hand suddenly slipped to the ground. "What should I do?" He stopped. Only the tips of the petals were left in his hand. The bee on the ground was covered with pollen. It buzzed and tried to fly, but could not. Still, the boy made no move. The honeybee buzzed again. This time it flew away, drawing circles as it rose up high in the sky. The boy did not follow the bee with his eyes as it disappeared; instead, he hurried toward the dwellings.

The squirrel buyer had stopped his bicycle in front of the boy's tent and was talking to the boy's father. I'm just in time, the boy thought. "Papa!"

"Stop talking nonsense," the squirrel buyer was saying. "You complain that ten *won* is too cheap for one squirrel, but to tell the truth, if I pay that I'll only make two *won* profit. Two *won* ! Do you know how much squirrels go for on Kanghwa Island? I can buy all I want there for a single *won* each." The squirrel man fanned his face in great gusts with his mountaineer's cap.

"Even so, if you take them to the city you can get at least thirty *won* apiece."

"How ridiculous! Who on earth told you such a

wild story? Why don't you go there yourself and see? You'd probably have a hard time selling a single squirrel, even if you spent the whole day."

The boy's father answered with an unsatisfied look. "When you send them over to Japan, can't you get a dollar apiece in western money?"

"Well, I don't know how much they bring in Japan, but it would take all kinds of trouble to send these squirrels there. They'd have to give each one shots, and prepare lightweight cages to ship them by air. And that's not all. Ten percent or more would die on the way, so if I sent a hundred, ten would be lost and . . ."

The boy's father showed no reaction. He stood staring at one spot.

The boy became impatient. "Papa . . ."

"Besides, they wouldn't just die of disease . . . I mean, some would kill each other. Since the shippers send them by plane, they're afraid of even the slightest extra weight so they don't put water in the cages. When the squirrels get thirsty they kill each other and suck the blood. It's hard to believe. Even tiny creatures do it. How do they know that there's blood inside another body . . . and that they can live by sucking it?"

The boy's father stood there silently in the same position. His face had lost the warm expression it had worn when the squirrel man arrived. "You think that's limited to squirrels? What about people? Anyway, give me twenty *won* each for them."

"This is crazy . . . You mean I should put out my own money to pay you? . . . invest my own money to no end? Now, at that last house over there, they sold them to me with no complaints. Why are you acting like this today?"

The squirrel man looked as though he were considering something. "Look, do you think this business of sending squirrels to Japan can continue forever? The Japanese have already started breeding Korean squirrels. And me . . . how much longer will it be before I can't even make a living at this? Just don't complain."

The squirrel man put his mountaineer's cap back on as if he had nothing more to say. He lifted the edge of the tent opening, then, without asking permission, picked up the family's squirrel cage and walked to his bicycle.

"So this time you've got four."

The boy's father said nothing.

The squirrel man moved aside the grass that covered the top of the wire cage on his bicycle rack. Then he lifted the four squirrel's inside. The new squirrels and the others already in the cage raised a fuss.

"Papa . . ."

The boy had wanted to speak before the squirrel man left, but his father just stood vacantly watching the other man's actions. Sweat shone on his father's face and neck. He had an absent look, but his face also had something uneasy about it. The boy could say nothing more so long as his father looked like this.

After he finished tying up the load, the squirrel man took four ten-*won* bills from his inner pocket and handed them to the boy's father, who took them without a word. Then the squirrel man weighed the other's stare. He picked a green pumpkin from the patch, broke it into several pieces, and placed them inside the cage. The boy looked up at his father. How strange he was today! It was a rule that the boy could not pick pumpkins for the squirrels they caught and kept in the house, but his father had said nothing at all when the squirrel man did it. He just stood there absent-mindedly.

Thinking that his father might like to hear about the squirrel he had seen on the hill, this time the boy grabbed his arm and shook it. "Papa, there's a squirrel up there."

Before he could respond the squirrel man asked where.

The boy pointed toward the hill in back of the tents.

"You mean it's caught in a trap?"

"No, I just saw it there."

"So you think it's still waiting there saying, 'Catch me, catch me'?"

"Well, it went into a hole . . ."

The boy's father, who had seemed indifferent to his son's words, picked up a long pole that was standing beside the tent. A horsehair noose was attached to the end.

He gave the boy a glance, as if to say, "Let's go." Half-running, the boy led the way. The squirrel man quickly picked up the family's woven cage and followed.

Not a word passed among them as they reached the place where the trees stood on the hill. When they arrived at a spot where they could see the hole beneath the tree stump, the boy gestured and nodded toward it. The father had the boy and the squirrel man stay behind while he approached the hole alone.

He stopped. He put the end of the pole into the hole and pulled it out two or three times. Then he put the snare at the mouth of the hole and held it motionless.

The squirrel did not appear.

"Are you sure it went in there?" the squirrel buyer asked impatiently.

The boy nodded.

"I don't think it's still there. It's probably already run off somewhere."

The boy, too, thought that was what had happened, but still his father stood immobile. Then, something popped out of the hole.

"There . . . ," the boy started to speak, but the squirrel man covered his mouth with his big hand.

The boy's father carefully moved the snare in front of the squirrel's nose. "Put on the crown. Put on the crown," he muttered, telling the squirrel to get into the noose. As if in response to his words, the squirrel played with the snare with its foreleg. Then, in a bound, the squirrel put its head through.

Determined not to miss this chance, the boy's father raised the pole. The squirrel wriggled in the air.

The squirrel man ran over immediately and put the struggling squirrel in the cage. "It's a female with young. The teats are full."

The boy, with his mouth covered by the buyer's hand, had tumbled backwards from the force of the man's movement as he had dashed over to the squirrel. With his great belly facing the sky, the boy could not get up easily, so he was unable to see the squirrel buyer put the snared animal into the cage. The boy hoisted himself to his feet with a sullen look.

"We'll have to catch a male, too, since you caught the female," the buyer said.

"Would we catch it as easily as this?"

The boy did not understand what was meant by "male" and "female."

As on their way up the hill, they went down without exchanging a word. The boy thought his father was limping more than usual on his bad leg.

The squirrel skittered about when the man put it in his wire cage. This time it seemed only the newcomer made a commotion.

The squirrel buyer gathered his load together again, and took two five-*won* coins from his pocket. He jingled them in the palm of his hand as he offered them to the boy.

"This is for the kid. It's just as if he caught the thing himself."

The boy gladly accepted the money. The coins felt cool in his palm. He grasped them tightly. Across his mind flashed the image of candies and sweets in the little shop further down the hill. But his father moved to take the money.

"Well, shall I give you a ride on my bicycle then?" The squirrel buyer took the boy under the armpits and lifted him onto the saddle.

He was a bit frightened.

"Hey, there's nothing to be scared of . . . nothing at all."

The man had the boy hold the handlebars while he pulled the bicycle along. It rattled. The boy was exhilarated, but he was disappointed that he could not show the other children. Why were there no children out, today of all days?

After he had pulled the bicycle for a while, the squirrel man said, "Why doesn't a big boy like you cover his little red pepper? Why, you're all belly." He stretched out his finger and snickered as he poked the boy sharply in the navel. He seemed to be in a good mood.

The boy also laughed. His whole face wrinkled.

"You watch that hole and see if another squirrel goes in there, okay?"

The boy nodded.

"If you do what I say, I'll give you another ride next time."

The boy nodded again, and the wrinkles once more filled his face when he smiled. The man stopped his bicycle at the end of the tents to let the boy off, then got on himself.

The boy stood there, his eyes following the bicycle as it wound along the narrow road and around the far side of a pile where women sat in clusters under the blazing sun sorting through the garbage. His mother was probably there, but he could not tell which one she was from this distance. The boy again turned his eyes toward the bicycle and followed it until it disappeared.

The boy thought about going inside the house to eat what pumpkin gruel might be left, but instead he started back up the hill. He stopped at the border of the sweet potato patch where the bindweed was blooming, and peed quickly.

His father was digging out rocks as before.

When he got to the place where the rugged stones stuck out, he rubbed the sole of his foot just a bit, then went on to where the trees stood.

He had no intention of looking for acorns, but went directly to the spot where he could see the hole beneath the stump. He watched it for a long time. His legs hurt, so he sat down. He thought of the joy of riding the bicycle. Next time I'll ask him to take me a little further, where Mama is.

Though he waited some time, there was no sign of a squirrel. He looked around, then crept toward the hole and peeped inside. He flinched. Something was wiggling in the pitch black of the hole. They were tiny, but they looked like squirrels. The boy put his hand inside and took them out. There were three in all.

The boy held them in both hands close to his chest and started to rush down the hill, but thinking he might drop the squirming babies if he ran, he slackened his pace.

As soon as he reached his father, he called out, "Papa, look at this!"

His father kept at his work. The boy could not tell if he had heard or not, so he quickly approached him.

"Look at this, Papa."

Only then did his father turn his head. He seemed surprised.

"Where did they come from?"

"I caught them."

"Where?"

"Right up there where we were before."

"What? In that hole?"

The boy was confused. He thought he would hear praise, but his father was shouting at him.

"Please sell them."

"Son, who would buy them?"

"We'll raise them until they're bigger. Then we'll sell them."

"What a fool! Stop your babbling. Hurry up and put them back where you found them."

The boy hesitated.

"Right now! Aren't you going to put them back? What would you feed them? These are newborns. Hurry and take them back there."

The boy finally seemed to realize the reason for his father's anger. He hurried away.

Oh, that's right. They have to have mother's milk. They'll have to have mother's milk soon. Then we can sell them when they're bigger. Then the squirrel man will take me even further on his bicycle, he thought.

The boy hugged the baby squirrels to his chest and headed up the path at a fast pace.

"Silly boy! He thinks he has to catch the male. What's he going to do? . . . use those as bait?"

For a moment, as he focused his gaze on his son's retreating figure, his eyes misted with tears.

*Translated by Martin Holman*

# The Night He Came Late

It was another fine brisk day in mid-autumn. The pleasantness of the day meant little to him, however, for, rain or shine, the weather could not affect his routine.

The alley he was passing was quiet as usual at ten o'clock in the morning. As he walked past a house surrounded by a stone wall he heard the sound of someone playing a piano – badly, as usual. Some child forced by grownups to practice must be pounding away at the keys. Walking on, he heard the dog start to bark. The dog never barked until he had already gone past the house. Perhaps it remembered to bark only when its ears caught the fading sound of a passerby's footsteps. He had never seen the dog, but he could tell from its bark that it was big. It seemed to bark not to protect the house from strangers but simply as a duty; therefore it sounded hollow and powerless.

Coming out of the alley into the street, he saw on the empty lot to his left the familiar dumping ground, with its eternal pile of trash. To his right was a cigarette shop. He went up to the shop and pushed a 500-*won* bill into the seller's window. The old man inside, putting his hand on a stack of cigarette packs, looked out as he had done many times before, "How many packs do you want?"

One, of course. He held up his index finger. The old man pushed out a pack with the change, which he had counted very slowly.

He shoved the money into his pocket. That was the first change he got out of the day's 4,000 *won* – the sum he got from his woman every day. Tearing off a corner of the pack, he took a cigarette, lit it and crossed the street toward the bus stop.

The bus was not crowded because the rush-hour was over, so he found a seat. After a few stops he closed his eyes. In the afternoon he felt quite strong but in the morning he was always exhausted. That seemed to be the way he was.

Voices coming from the seat in front woke him up. Two boys who looked like college students were talking.

"You son-of-a-bitch, shut your big mouth. She's a nice girl. . . . The only difficulty is she's too self-protective."

"But a girl like that can be easy if you hit on her vulnerable points."

"How?"

"Things have become so matter-of-fact nowadays, especially language. Use old-fashioned words, be gallant. Praise her to the skies. There are very few young people immune to flattery. Girls succumb to any praise they hear, even if they know it doesn't mean anything. It's worth trying. It's a female weakness that's very appealing. But be careful not to use clichés. Use your imagination!"

"How about a few examples?"

"Free of charge? I won't give you a sure-fire line unless you buy me some wine."

"You drive a hard bargain. But how do I know it's even worth listening to? You'd better give me an example."

"All right." He took out a small notebook from his pocket. "I'll give you my precious secret . . . . When you praise a girl's eyes, don't say, 'Your eyes are as bright as morning stars', the usual stuff. Instead, tell her, 'Your eyes are like the fully ripening grapes of Bordeaux.' Bordeaux is famous for its grapes. Or you could compare her eyes to the crystal clear water of Bach Lake in the Alps. Now let's move on to the mouth."

"But, hey, I can't remember all this. Why don't you lend me the book?"

"I'll lend it to you only after you give me wine, cheap or otherwise."

As the boy was putting his notebook back into his pocket, the other snatched it from him. A scuffle ensued.

"That notebook is full of my private secrets. Give it back, you bastard, or you'll be sorry!"

"When you give me some wine . . ." He left his seat and sprang off the bus.

"You rat, you're running away," the owner of the book shouted, chasing the other boy.

He closed his eyes again. The scene seemed to blur together with recent newspaper headlines announcing recurrent closings of colleges and universities because of student demonstrations.

Off the bus at Kwangwha Gate, he walked past the front gate of Duksoo Palace and into Seoul Precinct Court. He had made it a rule to visit this court every day. As usual several cars were parked there and people seemed to be walking with either faster or slower steps than elsewhere.

As was his habit, he walked steadily through the front of the court building, turned to the west and entered a public gallery. In the hall was the familiar sight of people looking for the courtroom they intended to visit and others complaining about postponed trial dates or bad choice of attorney. Every face betrayed tension and anxiety. He used to feel the same way in this place, but curious as well. Now he had become immune to such sentiments; all he wanted was to kill time.

The first door he tried opened on an empty courtroom. The next room was too crowded to get in. The third room had only a handful of people in the audience and he took a seat at the back. He used to be selective in his choice of trials, but now any trial would do, so long as a seat was available.

Of four defendants, one was just then being cross-examined by the prosecutor, who was saying that the defendant had been charged with using violence for the second time. The young man seemed to confess by his silence. Asked why he had beaten the plaintiff, inflicting serious injury despite no resistance, the defendant said the plaintiff's total submission had heightened his fury. To the question of whether he had been drunk at that time, the young man replied no. The audience stirred and muttered among themselves. The defendant also admitted that he had previously been convicted of assault committed for no other reason than that he had disliked his victim's face.

This stirred the audience once again. Most of them seemed sympathetic to the plaintiff. The judge, sitting in the center of the platform, signaled the audience to be quiet. Neither judge nor prosecutor seemed very concerned about the proceedings, speaking only out of habit. The audience, on the other hand, showed some genuine feeling.

The bully on trial was ordered to sit down and the next defendant told to stand. He looked about the same age as the other three – barely over twenty. After some routine questioning the prosecutor accused him of having committed the same offense for the third time. The defendant, apparently acknowledging his guilt, dropped his head.

"You saw the plaintiff withdrawing money from the bank and you followed him to the subway in order to steal his wallet, didn't you?" the prosecutor demanded.

The young man raised his head and replied that was not the case, that he had felt the fat wallet pressed against his hand in the crowded train, that it was sheer accident and that he had intended to move his hand but, pushed by the crowd, he couldn't and so he couldn't help taking the wallet.

The onlookers were quiet. No one seemed convinced by the young man. The judge sat dully, having no need to admonish the audience this time. What a boring job it must be. He remembered that, at the previous day's trial, one of the members of the judicial panel trying a civil debt case had constantly pretended to wipe his lips, in an effort to conceal his yawns. Although still young, he was already bored with his job, perhaps with the entire legal profession.

The noise of creaking benches and voices caused him to stir. The audience was moving toward the back door. He heard someone saying that the next trial would be held in three weeks. He must have been dozing.

Next he went into a coffee shop across the street from the court. This shop was usually crowded by people connected in some way with the law. Taking a seat in the middle of the room he ordered coffee and started smoking cigarettes as though to make up for lost time.

With his cigarettes and coffee, paying no attention to his surroundings, he thought hard about what he should eat for lunch: Korean, Chinese or Japanese dishes, or a western meal? Broiled beef with rice, broiled ribs with rice, *sulungtang* [1], beef-knuckle soup, *naengmyon* [2], beef chop suey, *samsun jajahng* [3], *ulmyon* [4], *jungol* [5] with rice, puff-fish soup with rice, *susi* [6], beefsteak, hamburger, beef cutlets, or pork cutlets? He gave this great thought because his woman, in bed, never failed to ask him what he had

1. *sulungtang*: a hot soup containing slices of beef, scallions and boiled rice.
2. *naengmyon*: a bowl of cold buckwheat noodles with vegetables, meat, and red pepper.
3. *samsun jajahng*: hot noodles with a salty dark-brown gravy consisting of diced vegetables and pork.
4. *ulmyon*: noodles with vegetables in a hot, sour, and starchy broth.
5. *jungol*: tripe with vegetables cooked at the table.
6. *susi*: compressed pieces of boiled rice seasoned with mustard and each covered by a slice of raw fish, which may then be dipped lightly in soy sauce.

for lunch. She seemed to think that what he had eaten for lunch directly affected his ability to please her in her boudoir. So what should he choose for his lunch today?

He finally decided on dog meat stew, a reputed aphrodisiac and something he hadn't eaten for a long time. The last time he told his woman that he'd eaten dog meat for his midday meal she made a face, but then said softly that she always wondered how dogs could remain together mating for such a long time. Then she became hot, perhaps inspired by the thought.

Glancing at his watch, he left the tea shop and walked to the dog-stew restaurant in Sumwha Lane. This shop was famed for its quality meat and for the fact that, unlike other dog-stew restaurants, it stayed open throughout the year, and not only in the summer season. He ordered a heaping plate of meat and a bowl of stew into which he put steamed rice before eating.

Afterwards, he walked toward the second block of Ulchi Street, this time headed toward the office of his friend who worked at a trading company. Not so much to see him as to sit on the sofa in one corner of the room. They had been friends in high school and in college, now some ten years ago. They continued to meet very frequently even after their school days and, as a matter of fact, he went to his friend's office almost every workday.

They didn't talk much. More often than not, no word passed between them during his visit. This friend was not hampered by his presence. Regardless of whether his friend was in or not, he could go right into the office and head for the familiar sofa where he could make himself at home, browsing through the financial section of the newspaper, especially the stock market report. He left when he felt like it, without bothering to say goodbye. Nevertheless, their eyes occasionally exchanged farewells.

On this day his friend was not in the office and, as was sometimes the case, the sofa was occupied by a stranger. Knowing where to find his friend, he went up to the roof of the high-rise office building, where five or six people had formed a circle and were tossing a volleyball back and forth. Leaning against the railing on the border of the court, he watched them playing, thinking what poor players they were. But, as if in defiance of his judgment, they managed to keep the ball in the air for quite a long time until his friend hit what appeared to be an easy ball too hard. It rose high up above them and went over the railing.

While everybody's eyes were following the ball through the air in amazement, his friend started grinning as if he had done something wonderful. For a moment his humdrum life had been relieved. Avoiding his friend's eyes, which were now directed consciously at him, he turned around to leave. Descending the staircase, he thought he might visit Changgyung Zoo to see his favorite white bear.

The white bear was pacing intently back and forth in its cage, vigorously nodding its head. He watched the bear from his usual bench at some distance from the cage. The bear, with occasional pauses, repeated its exercises, oblivious of spectators. It too was seeking relief from life's tedium. He had read an article in a foreign magazine about a caged gorilla that throws up its meals and eats them again as many as thirty times between its regular feeding times, and a chimpanzee that suddenly rises up and claps its hands to draw the attention of spectators huddled in front of its cage. It then throws shit all over them, just to have some fun in a life which is otherwise unbearably boring.

Monkeys will masturbate, or pluck out all their hair as far as their hands can reach, until they become almost entirely bald. Lionesses will give up breeding or even devour their cubs. It was once reported in the newspaper that a male tiger bit its mate to death in this very zoo. These wild beasts could not seem to accommodate themselves to the comforts by which others controlled their lives.

After the zoo he browsed in the bookshops on Chungmu Street with little thought of buying anything, and then proceeded to a cellar coffee house a few doors from the last bookshop he had left. This coffee house generally had customers of all ages and occupations, all trying to look avant-garde, but gradually the inner half of the room had been taken over by university students while the outer half was relegated to older people. As time went on, however, the youngsters were coming to occupy the whole room, driving away the others. The music had changed accordingly from alternating selections of quiet and popular music to a steady stream of rock.

He was no longer as young as most of those present but neither was he as old as the older patrons, so he could sit anywhere in the middle, near the boundary.

Today, however, he felt slightly uncomfortable, as if he were swimming in a strange pool. But since the young people did not seem to think him too old he decided not to worry. It was simply a place to kill time.

A young woman, apparently a student, came up to his table and spoke to the collegiate boy sitting next to him, "You ask me to come and then you sit in this obscure corner . . . . I was about to leave because I couldn't see you."

The young man snickered. "But this is the most prestigious table in the whole house, fit to receive honorable guests. Do sit down."

"May I ask your name?" the boy said when the girl was seated. "It'd be nice if we knew each other's names."

"Why not just call me 'you'?" the girl replied quickly.

"In that case my name'll have to be 'you' too."

She chuckled and when the boy proposed that they exchange student ID cards, she said, "So that we can compare credentials?"

Glancing at his watch, he got up from the table. Paying at the counter, he noted the young couple leaving. They didn't seem to mind skipping the coffee at their rendezvous and were evidently satisfied with each other's credentials.

Outside the cellar door and starting up the stairs, he saw the girl, who had gone behind, pressing the boy's back with her fingers. The boy stood still. The girl slipped her hand in his and they walked up together side by side, taking up the whole of the narrow staircase. They reminded him of the two students he had seen on the bus that morning. Similar scenes could be seen more often now that the universities had been shut down. He smiled, neither sweet nor bitter.

Outside it was dusk.

When he opened the door of the gambling joint he was greeted by the usual cacophony of metal from the slot machines, by the smoky air and the sight of people pulling handles or just watching. The players, though looking cool, were seething inside with the excitement of losing or winning.

As was his custom, he got fifty chips for five hundred *won* at the booth, went to an unoccupied machine in the middle and put a chip into the slot, pulling the handle. The machine clicked and whirled and three designs turned up one after another; they did not match. He lost, as he would do many times more. As he went on, however, he had better luck and won almost a dozen chips. He saw the man next to him leaving in a dejected mood, having lost all his chips. The vacant machine was instantly taken over by another player.

He was there to pass time, not to win, so he did not mind losing. In fact losing was what he wanted. Still, he did not want to lose all his chips too quickly because that would mean he would have to leave before the allotted time. It was agreed that he should not lose more than fifty chips. As for winning, it was not his role to gain, but to spend.

This time, before he could run out of chips, he hit two watermelons and one star; the machine yielded 1,500 *won* in coins. As he had done once before with a jackpot of 2,000 *won*, he changed all the money for chips and fed several slots simultaneously to save time. Pull the handle . . . click and whirl . . .

The unexpected win caused some delay in his routine, the next step of which was stopping in at the *sul chip*. He drank *chongju* * in a glass with simple food. He preferred this wine because his woman did not like the smell of *soju* and he himself had grown to dislike the taste of *makkŏlli*. He had stopped drinking beer soon after he graduated from college.

Smoking a cigarette and sipping *chongju*, he fell to thinking about how to please his woman in bed tonight. When she came to him he should refrain from kissing her on the lips, in case she could smell the dog meat he had eaten. Instead, he would move his lips behind her earlobes and then to the valley between her breasts. This time his tongue would participate in the action while his hands would lightly stroke her. The woman would not allow him to nibble at the nipples, nor would she let him fondle her plump breasts, for she was very much afraid that they might lose their shape, even a little.

She had given birth to a child but had not breast-fed it, so she had been able to retain her figure, by which she set great store. He had no idea whose baby it was, whether it was a boy or girl, or even whether it was dead or alive, and, if alive, where it was placed, for she had never mentioned it to him, nor had he bothered to ask. At any rate it should be regarded as a matter for pride that a woman of thirty-three, whether she had had a baby or not, was equipped with such a

* *chongju*: clear, refined rice wine.

voluptuous bosom. Accordingly, he felt the necessity of being especially careful in handling her breasts. For instance, he let go of them ungrudgingly as soon as the nipples hardened.

As he savored his second glass of wine, he continued to toy with the image of himself searching out the areas of her body which could give her new erotic pleasure, studying the most effective ways of inducing it. It was his duty to explore her body and to perfect his skill in exciting her.

Although he was not supposed to be engaged in any productive activities during the day, he considered it essential for him to become a most capable man in rendering service to his woman. For that reason he had gone through many a sexual guide, as well as a lot of pornography. But on the whole they had nothing new in them and were of little help. A peculiar feature of Korean pornography was that, while women exposed themselves boldly without any inhibition, even smiling as they did so, men revealed their fear either by wearing dark glasses or by twisting their necks unnaturally to hide their faces.

Yes, women were bolder than men in bed and encouraged men to experiment. Why then couldn't he explore his woman's body further and discover yet another pleasure-giving spot? After quite a long search in his imagination, his fingers came to a halt, for they found one such spot at last at the tail bone. Yes, he should stroke it with his tongue and see her reaction.

Lighting another cigarette, he ordered a third glass of wine. This was to be his last, for she would not like him to drink more and get drunk. Besides, he did not want to lose his potency, a possibility taught by experience. His potency, he felt, was waning of late, and not as a result of alcohol. While he was still intent on foreplay, his erection died in spite of himself. Getting anxious about it only worsened the condition.

It did not, however, follow that he should omit foreplay, which she liked immensely. When she noticed what was wrong with him, she chuckled and, calling his penis "your lovely snail," held it with her elastic fingers, making various efforts to revive the shrunken thing. Needless to say, the longer it took to accomplish her purpose, the more face he lost. The saving grace, even on such occasions, was that she would become hot in the process.

When she thought that he was going to come too fast, she often suggested that he should smoke. This he did. After smoking he would resume his act, perhaps feigning ejaculation. That, he learned, served to speed up her climaxes. It was his duty to make every effort to please her without regard to his own satisfaction. She embraced him so hard that she almost feared her treasured breasts might get crushed, but between the surges of joy which she felt inside she would tease him, gasping, "You want me to let go of you, don't you?"

Then he would say, "Not at all," and would hold her sweating body tight against his own until her last surge had completely calmed. It was hard labor on his part. He was certain that during their pillow talk before copulation tonight she would bring up the subject of how long dogs can prolong their mating. In that case he would be wiser if he changed the subject to horses, telling her as vividly as possible about how they go about the act, as if he had seen it with his own eyes. But he should not forget to add that it was less time-consuming than with dogs.

He glanced at his watch and finishing up his wine, asked for the bill. It was an unwritten law between the two of them that he should return home neither later nor earlier than 10:30. When the change was brought to him he took only enough for his bus fare home and handed the remainder back to the waitress as a tip, the amount varying according to how much he had spent for lunch that day. At any rate he was not supposed to have even a single *won* when he returned home. He was to spend all the 4,000 *won* she gave him every day. She never asked him how he had spent the money, and he never asked her how she earned it.

On the empty lot at the entrance to the alley leading to her house he noticed a fire burning. He had never seen a fire there before. As he approached he saw that it was burning trash, fed by several youngsters. The flames flickered, lightening and darkening the surrounding figures. He stopped before realizing he had done so, and stood staring at the fire. Strangely, the flames looked black. . . .

All of a sudden he saw a grey mist engulfing the space before his eyes. Looming in the mist was a ravine in which magnolias blossomed profusely, emitting a strong fragrance which assaulted his nose. The full moon glowed above. Then he heard the murmurings of familiar student voices, followed by the sight of a youthful crowd at a campfire. They formed a circle around the fire and started singing in chorus and dancing, kicking the air. Singing songs of protest and dancing, holding one another by the shoulders, they became increasingly violent. Now they were calling out, acclaiming their leader . . . It was himself at the age of . . . .

The mist disappeared from his sight as suddenly as it had appeared and the flickering flames of the burning trash reappeared. It was dying down, darkening the place. Using a pair of tongs with professional skill, one of the young men picked up something from a big basket behind him and placed it on the fire. The flames rose again. Then they looked black once more. He halted, for he thought one of the faces of the three young rag-pickers vaguely resembled one of his comrades who had died many years before. He had seen that youth dying, fatally wounded, shedding blood, and the blood he remembered was bright red. He realized that he had been living for years now in a world where everything looked either black or white. Even the flames now looked black instead of yellow or orange.

He walked up to the young men, squatted before the fire, put out his hands as they did, and spoke. "It's getting chilly, isn't it?"

The rag-pickers ignored him, thinking he was drunk, but he insisted: "How's business? How much money do you make in a day?"

They looked bored and did not bother to answer. The boy who resembled his dead friend finally broke the silence. "Each of us makes six or seven hundred *won* a day, but some get up to a thousand. Does that satisfy your curiosity?"

"I see," he nodded, "but why don't you go home and stop hanging around here so late?"

Another young man, who was feeding the fire with rags from his basket, answered bluntly, "We can't use our room until they vacate it half an hour before the midnight curfew."

"Who?"

"Guys who come with women to rent the rooms for a few hours."

"You live there because it's cheaper?"

They did not speak further. Only the fire made any noise, flames rising and falling as it flickered out. Then the third boy rose and the other two followed suit. As if they had tacitly agreed upon their next step, they unbuttoned their army pants and urinated on the cinders.

He rose too and, stepping forward to join them, opened his fly and started pissing. He was thinking he could pawn his wristwatch to get money and check into the rooming house tonight with them. Then laughter poured out from deep inside him. The night air vibrated with it as it spread out a great distance. It was big laughter, free and unrestricted. He had not laughed like that for a long time.

The boys seemed to think him helplessly drunk. He watched as they silently shouldered their baskets, took up their rag-picking tongs and walked away.

*Translated by Chang Wang-rok*

# In a Small Island Village

Seven-year-old Ugi had gone down to the shore to set adrift a piece of pine bark shaped like a boat. The waves were rather strong in the west wind, and each time they washed up toward him, Ugi watched the boat to see how it would be dragged under the water. Some time ago, the boat on which Ugi's father was working was caught by heavy seas and sunk. As in most cases, the body was never found. And now, in his own way, Ugi was trying to play out that moment.

On the beach six-year-old Chini was squatting before a seaweed doll. She was pounding the surface of the sand with both hands and wailing as if in lamentation. "Aigo, aigo, aigo," she sang out her dirge. Chini's father had also gone to sea with Ugi's, also never to return. She was imitating the way her mother had grieved. Chini's darkly tanned chest, left bare by her clothes, was flat as a boy's.

"What a fit you're throwing." Ugi walked up beside the girl.

"Someday, when you die, I'll cry like this for you." Chini looked up at Ugi. Her eyes were unlike those of a child; they were misty like the distant light from the ocean.

"I won't die, but if you want to, you little shrimp, go ahead."

Ugi trampled on the doll, crushing it. Then he scampered off.

Chini gazed at Ugi's tanned back, which glistened in the sunlight as he ran away. Then she stood up and walked around the edges of a net that had been spread out on the sloping sand to be dried and repaired. It was better than walking on the sand because the net was not as hot. She enjoyed the ticklish sensation on the soles of her feet.

Ugi had returned, behind Chini's back, and he gave her a sudden shove. She tumbled sideways. Then Ugi nimbly tossed the net over her and scurried off again. Chini squirmed and kicked to free herself from the net, but the more she tried, the more entangled she became.

The summer Ugi turned eleven and Chini ten, the Turtle Rock was a frequent playground for the mischievous boys. It was shaped like a giant turtle crawling up onto the land from the sea.

When the boys jumped off the back of the Turtle Rock, Ugi always swam the farthest. They leapt into the water again and again without a rest. Then, tired from swimming, the boys would bet on who could stay underwater the longest. The only time Ugi lost was at these diving contests.

One day, however, after several rounds of diving, Ugi did not reappear, although the rest of the boys had all come up. One boy struck the back of the Turtle Rock with a stone, shouting down into the water, "Get out, damn you! Right now! That's enough!" But no sign appeared from beneath the waves. Suddenly one boy picked up his shorts and began to run toward the village. Then all the others turned pale with fear, grabbed their shorts, and ran after him.

A little way off, Chini was digging clams. Seeing the boys' expressions, she called loudly, asking what had happened. But the boys ran on without answering. As soon as she realised that Ugi was not among them, Chini tossed aside her bamboo basket and raced toward the Turtle Rock. No sooner did she reach it than she jumped into the sea. Ugi was under the water, just as she had thought. She found him immediately. He was holding fast to a rock beneath the surface, not stirring. Since he would not disengage his arms, which were wrapped around the rock, she was barely able to pull him free. When she dragged him up to the beach he looked unmistakably dead.

Chini was clutched by fear, but without thinking she began to suck Ugi's nose to remove the water. She remembered once seeing a grown-up do this to a drowned boy. Chini sucked and spat and sucked again. Now it was no longer distasteful or frightening.

Chini was sucking and spitting frantically when suddenly a gurgling sound came from Ugi's throat. She sucked at his mouth. His chest moved, and a vapor flowed from between his lips. Again and again he vomited water. Chini turned his head to one side to make it easier for him to spit up. Then she waited for him to open his eyes. She watched his chest rising and falling, and for the first time her eyes moved below his stomach where he had nothing on. His small member stood out moving by itself. Quickly

Chini picked up Ugi's tattered shorts and tossed them over him.

Seeing villagers in the distance swarming towards her, Chini began to run back to where she had left her basket.

Just like her mother and all the other village women, Chini had to live with the knowledge that the men had to go to sea when they turned seventeen. Feelings of loss and sorrow were out of the question.

The more Ugi had been to sea, the more muscular his build became and the rougher his face grew from the salt. Only on the nights they slept together, when he was home from the sea, could Chini regard him as her husband. That alone satisfied her.

Three years had not passed since Ugi first went out to sea when he began to grow unhappy with their meager catch. He complained incessantly when he returned from sea, "It's no good using rowboats. We have to get a motorboat and go far out to sea." These grumblings pierced Chini's breast. Ugi seemed to be a man driven mad by the sea, dreaming only a desperate dream of going far out in the ocean. Chini's feelings changed until she could no longer think of Ugi as her husband even when they slept together.

She wanted somehow to bring Ugi's heart back. If only she could have a baby. If she did, Ugi would forget his vain ideas of going out to the distant sea. Then she could have him look after the child when he was in the village, like other husbands. How wonderful it would be then, to be able to tend to some of the work outside. But this was not something that would turn out as she desired.

Eventually it happened that sometimes Ugi would not return with the others when he went out to sea. He stayed on other islands, then came back several days late each time, looking as though he were about to die. After he got home, he would do nothing but mutter about motorboats.

One night Chini heard someone calling from outside. It was Ugi's voice, the voice of her husband, who had been away at sea for several days. She opened the door quickly. No one was there. The late autumn moon, just past full, shone down unobstructed.

Maybe he's beyond the wall, Chini thought. She went out to look, but saw not so much as the shadow of anyone. Chini stood in the moonlight gazing about for a moment. Then, as she was about to go back inside, she heard Ugi's voice calling again. This time it came from the direction of the nettle tree not far from the house. She ran to see, but she could find no trace of a person. Nothing was there except the leafless branches of the tree drawing sharp, tangled shadows in the moonlight. Again she tried to go back to the house, but once more Ugi's voice called. This time it came from about ten or twelve yards ahead, though she could not quite determine the location. When she went to where she thought she had heard the voice, however, the sound withdrew about the same distance from her. Chini passed by the grove of camellias and walked to the strip of sand, then on to the shore. The light of the moon was full on the ocean as well, and the myriad ripples in the water glimmered like the scales of a fish. And there, about the same distance out in the sea, Ugi's voice called out to Chini.

She got into a boat nearby and set out into the sea, drifting about here and there, following the voice in the moonlight. She never once doubted her ears or thought it odd that Ugi's voice should be heard there.

The next morning a villager discovered Chini collapsed in a boat far from shore. She was six months pregnant at the time.

"It wasn't until later that I found out what had happened. They had been fishing near Kŏmun Island, but hadn't caught anything, so they were to come back. They say Ugi alone wanted to go further out. He was so insistent that the others on the boat could do nothing to stop him. That night the moon had been shining brightly there too, but after he went out in the boat, they say a strange storm blew in."

The woman who kept the tavern paused for a moment. "I couldn't even cry. If only he'd been in a motorboat, then even a big storm would have been no problem."

I looked at her eyes. They were like the misty light off the ocean, but her gaze was fixed on one spot. I saw no expression of emotion in her eyes that might match her words.

Not far away grew a single nettle tree, casting its dense shade, and some distance from there a grove of camellias stood in black shadow. Beyond that was a strip of sand from which the water spread out. A rather large fishing boat had returned from the sea to avoid the typhoon for which warnings were out and was moored at the shore. It was a motorboat, and most of its white paint had peeled off. Ahead lay a long island shaped like a horse's back, which cut off the way south. The east, moreover, was occupied by islands of various sizes, so this was an adequate place to take refuge from a southern or eastern wind, but it offered no shelter from the west. Despite the typhoon warning, the sapphire waters of the sea, oil floating on its surface, stretched out quietly in the distance as though the storm would never come this far.

Out to the left, at a bend in the wide curving shoreline stood the Turtle Rock. Viewed from here it was nothing more than a crag jutting out to the sea. Now a great number of young Ugi's were playing on the rock, diving and swimming. Closer in this way young Chini's were digging clams.

I lit a cigarette and asked the tavern woman something I had been hesitating to inquire about. "Are you living alone now?"

I was not asking if she had remarried. When she had lost her husband at sea she was six months pregnant. I was wondering about the baby she had been carrying.

"I live with my son."

I felt she had been fortunate.

"He's fifteen now. The years have passed so quickly. It's hard to believe he's that old."

The woman looked out at the sea. Her unwavering gaze was misty and calm.

"That's him over there. He's been swimming like that all morning."

I had not noticed earlier, but someone was in the water near the motorised fishing boat. As I looked out at him, he dove, and instantly bobbed up on the opposite side of the boat.

"Something might happen . . . him swimming like that." I frowned, thinking there could be trouble if he were accidentally caught under the boat.

"That's right, but whenever that kind of boat comes in, he always dives around it like that."

With my head turned toward the sea, I thought about her son being fifteen.

"Your son can't go out fishing yet, can he?" I asked.

The woman was silent for a moment. "He always pesters me wanting to, but I won't let him."

Now I understood why she had to run this small tavern.

After a moment the woman continued to speak, serenely, as though to herself.

"When he sees a big boat like that he makes a fuss wishing he could ride in it, but I was hoping to get him away from the water. Still, whatever I do, I can't keep him from it forever. These days I even think that the night his father drew me outside, he was not actually calling me; he was luring the baby inside me to the sea."

I was startled to hear a woman talk as she did on this remote island.

Her son was diving underwater as if he would pass beneath the bottom of the boat again. Even from this distance, I could see the rippling circles in the water following one on another.

*Translated by Martin Holman*

# Shadows of a Sound

Two boys ringing a bell. Actually the bellringer, the father of one of the boys, stood pulling the rope, while the children, who were moving their arms and bodies as the man did, merely grasped the end. Still, the children were just as elated as if they were ringing it themselves.

The peculiar rhythm of it – in the pause between the clanging sound when the rope was pulled and the gong-like sound when it was released, and in the longer interval before the next clang. This repeating pattern produced a lingering undertone that complemented the sound of the bell itself.

The rickety belfry was nothing but two tall, straight larchwood pillars facing each other. The bell was suspended from a crossbar placed on the top of the pillars and the rusty, peaked tin roof rested above like an overturned funnel. The whole tower shook when the bell was rung.

The bell rope was always tied up high on the pillar where only an adult on tiptoe could reach it. This was to keep the village children from playing with it. Still there were mischievous boys who shinnied up, untied the rope, and brought it down to ring the bell. The church members, however, were not deceived;

they knew from the rhythm of the bell when someone was playing a prank. One day the regular bellringer was away from home and the pastor tried to ring the bell himself. But ring though he would, the members, thinking it was those rascal children again, did not heed the call to worship. After that the pastor let the two boys take the bellringer's place whenever he was gone.

I received word that my childhood friend Sŏng'il had died. As my memories of him revived dimly through the flow of over forty years, what came back, resounding unexpectedly in my chest, was the dying echo of that bell. Then something else interrupted the bell's sound.

One Wednesday or Sunday evening, we two boys were to ring the bell in place of Sŏng'il's father for some reason or another. We pulled the rope, but no sound came; the clapper had been tied up against the crossbar. Someone was obviously playing a prank. The two of us managed with difficulty to carry a ladder to the tower and lean it against the pillar. Then Sŏng'il climbed up to untie the clapper. When he got all the way to the top, he gestured vigorously for me to come up, too. I wondered what had happened.

At a distance from the belfry, across some vacant land, stood the church elder's house surrounded by a stone wall. I climbed the ladder and looked beyond the wall where Sŏng'il was pointing. There, under the blossoming apricot tree in the rear garden where the evening shadows had fallen, we could see two dogs locked together back to back. One was the elder's Pekingese, and the female was a dog several times

larger, that I had never seen before. The strange dog
was walking forward, so the Pekingese was being
dragged along, unable to keep its rear legs on the
ground. The two of us burst into giggles. This
Pekingese was mean. Though we saw it all the time
and the dog knew us, every time we passed in front of
the house, it would come out to yap and chase us. If
we gestured as if fetching a rock to throw at it, the
dog would run away, only to snap at us again when we
turned around. Now, this dog, unable to keep its rear
feet on the ground, was being dragged incongruously
along. It was so ridiculous we snickered, unable to
contain ourselves.

All of a sudden we heard a shout from below. The
elder himself was glaring up at us furiously from the
base of the belfry. Before I realized what I was doing, I
wrapped my arms around the pillar and slid down.
The elder then moved the ladder, so Sŏng'il ended up
falling the distance. I merely got splinters from the
larch wood in my hands and arms, but Sŏng'il was
cursed by this fall: he became a hunchback.

Sometime after that, my family moved to Kwangju. I
was nine years old at the time.

I do not have what you might call a home town.
Until I was six, I lived somewhere that does not
remain in my memory. Then I lived in the village
where Sŏng'il was until I was nine. After that, we
passed through such places as Kwangju, Yŏng'in, and
Paju before finally settling in Seoul. There was
nothing to do but move about here and there
following my father, an elementary school teacher.

If the word "bellringer" had not been written

below Sŏng'il's name on the death notice, I would not have realized who the man was.

In these forty-odd years we had never even corresponded, much less seen each other. How did Sŏng'il know of me?

The village where Sŏng'il had lived was now off the National Highway about halfway between Suwŏn and Inch'ŏn. The recollections of when I was a nine-year-old child here were something I couldn't really connect with the place. Over forty years of changes gave me the impression that this was a completely different village. There were electric lights where there had been none before. A grocer, a potter, a pharmacy, and a barber shop all stood on the main street, so it seemed better now to call it a small town. Maybe it was because of the troops stationed on the outskirts that it had changed so much.

The elementary school on the right side of the street, a clapboard building before, was now made of concrete. I turned down the road beside the playground. Even the earth, muddy from the snow the day before and trampled by all kinds of feet, had changed from the red color I remembered.

As I looked toward a small rise behind the school at the square-shaped stone church in front of me, I had already lost any special feelings I had toward it. I could not expect the church alone to avoid change and remain as it was. Long ago it had been an old, traditional L-shaped house with a tile roof. It was arranged so the women sat in one branch of the "L" and the men in the other. While giving the sermon the pastor could not look at either side squarely, for the pulpit was in the angle of the "L" facing the inside corner.

Of course the bell tower was also different now. It stood to one side of the church. A cross with a lightning rod attached stood at the peak of the pointed roof, inscribing a distinct line in the clear winter sky. This scene, however, brought me no special recollections. I had not traveled this road groping for reminiscences or nostalgia. I merely let the memories surface as they would.

Within the outer wall of the church was the pastor's residence. Originally the roof had been thatched, now it was tiled. The old pastor had been a good fisherman. Whenever he had a spare moment, he took his net in hand and, instead of visiting his flock, went down to the stream in front of the village. The adults had called him Reverend Fisherman.

The current pastor was much younger. He looked about thirty or so. As soon as he learned who I was, he said the funeral had been held several days earlier. He also told me that Sŏng'il had asked him before he died to be sure to inform me of his death and emphasized that he should be referred to as the bellringer.

My coming here, then, did not even coincide with the funeral. The notice had been addressed to the school, but school was out of session at the time, so ten days had passed before the message made its roundabout way to me.

I asked the pastor where Sŏng'il's family lived. That would have to be the main purpose in coming. My childhood friend, lost in the tide of over forty years – this friend I had played with as a boy for no more than two or three years – he even knew my current place of employment. An indescribable impression grew on me that Sŏng'il had been watching me all my life. This would not let me leave without looking up his family. The young pastor's answer, however, frustrated my intentions. He had no family whatsoever. I could not have imagined Sŏng'il's hunchbacked shape in adulthood, but one must presume simply that he was so deformed he could not have a family.

The young pastor pointed to the place where Sŏng'il had lived alone until he died. It was a small room attached to the main gate. The loneliness and then the pain that this man had borne for over forty years surged into my breast. Although one may say that I am not totally responsible, that I cannot shoulder the burden for another man's misfortune, I felt a flash of remorse that accused me of being nothing more than an indifferent bystander. But what use was it to regret my error? Now there was nothing to do but visit the deceased man's grave before I returned home.

The young pastor seemed to recall something. He went into Sŏng'il's room and came out carrying a rather bulky roll of papers. The pastor told me that these were pictures Sŏng'il had taken pleasure in drawing during his lifetime. I did not recall that he had liked to draw when he was a child. Anyway, Sŏng'il had lived without a family, making these drawings his companions.

The pictures were drawn on paper with charcoal pencil. As I turned over the drawings one at a time, I thought I detected a common element in the simple lines. It was something that burned within the drawings. Sparks bounded from the entangled tree roots and from every bent and curved line. The countless mouths of the church faithful in the drawings spouted fire as they sang hymns, and flames rose even over the rugged stones jutting from the sides of the bald mountains.

Leafing through the pictures, I reached one in particular that I passed over more quickly than the others. After I had looked through them all, I asked the young pastor if I might take one of them with me as a memento. Having found the drawing I had leafed past hurriedly just a moment earlier, I rolled it up and put it in my overcoat pocket. Then I left.

Even the house where the elder had lived long ago was now a refined, modern Western-style house with a brick wall surrounding it. I walked around the wall and looked at the nameplate on the gate. A man named Kim was living there. It appeared the previous owner had been superceded. The elder long ago was not a Kim. Memory is a curious thing; it cannot be trusted. Though I could not recall what the elder's name was, I was quite certain it was not Kim.

But now, what did it matter what the elder's name was, or whether his descendants still lived there?

The common burial ground was almost directly across the street from the church on a ridge. Snow-covered gravestones were spread all over it, some reaching higher than others, but I could not distinguish which was the new mound. I thought I had made a mistake not asking the pastor earlier where the grave was located; nevertheless, I entered the graveyard, treading across the unspoiled snow. Looking around, I finally caught sight of a new wooden cross at the far end of the cemetery.

It was Sŏng'il's grave-marker. But, stand though I did in front of it, I could grasp nothing of the essence of the man. The only thing I could revive was the gaunt figure of a boy, his face veiled with suffering. A kind of rage suffused me. It was like the rage that entered my head when I first saw the drawing I now had rolled up in my pocket. The grave of the elder whose name I could not remember probably lay somewhere among these stones, but I could grasp nothing of his essence either through these forty years of changes. Now the only thing left in my memory was the shout and the furious expression of that middle-aged man as he glared up toward the top of the belfry.

I walked down the hill and checked the station schedule. A bus came every thirty minutes. I had some time before the next one, so I went into a teahouse. A few people sat around the stove in the middle of the room. Business seemed slack. I took a seat at a bright window.

Having taken only a sip of the tea that was brought, I pushed the cup away. Then I pulled the drawing out of my overcoat pocket and unrolled it. In the picture were two dogs. The smaller Pekingese, its hind legs in mid-air, was being dragged along by a larger dog. There were sparks here, too, just as in the other drawings. From the rendering of these animals, it seemed this crippled man had spewed forth these flames, unable to endure the torment of his deformity. Rage surged in me anew toward the punishment one middle-aged man had senselessly inflicted on this innocent boy, marring his life.

But my rage was nothing at all compared with the lonely, dark years of the dead man. After all this, why had Sŏng'il gone to work as a bellringer after his father?

When the waitress brought some green tea, I spoke

to her. "Excuse me. Can you hear the church bell clearly from here?" I wanted to tell her that the sound of the bell must have changed since the old days.

"Isn't today Saturday?" The waitress looked at me as though I was confused and thought it was Sunday. I had asked a futile question.

The people would surely have become accustomed to the sound of the new bellringer, so it made no difference. It was sufficient for me alone always to cherish the sound of the old one.

As I pondered these things, suddenly a bell began to sound within me.

Two boys were ringing it. This time Sŏng'il's father was not there, just the two boys alone pulling the rope together. In the interval between the clang when they pulled the rope and the gong when they released it, then in the longer interval before the next clang, as this clang and gong repeated, a peculiar trailing sound welled up – beneath, yet essential to the melody. The reverberations, like ripples on the water, filled my heart.

At that moment I saw something. The drawing before me seemed extraordinarily transformed. No, not transformed, it would be correct to say that at last I was able to discern the intentions of the dead Sŏng'il in drawing these pictures. Could working with a brush indeed have been so pleasant? Each of the lines that had looked to me like sparks were, in reality, the rhythms that sprang from unbearable delight. Our pure, innocent giggling came back to life, permeating every pencil mark, and we were able to share our laughter of forty years ago.

*Translated by Martin Holman*

# The Weighted Tumbler

Here is an old man who lives alone. A very old man, Yun is, known to his neighbors only as Uncle Medal. Once, while drinking in the tavern just across from the railroad tracks, he had boasted of the medal awarded his dead son. This son, an electrician, had gone to the war with the Army Signal Corps and was killed while trying to save several of his fellow soldiers. For this deed he was awarded a medal of distinction. However, none of the neighbors has seen the medal, nor the certificate presented to his family.

Alone in his dim room, old man Yun smiles to himself. Deep wrinkles fan out from the corners of his eyes. In his half-open mouth the dark space of four missing teeth stands out.

The tumbler, which has just rolled across the floor, wobbles back and forth as it rights itself. How much time he has spent making this toy! He does not have the skill to make it as fine as he would wish; he has no special tools to work with, only the knife he always carries with him in his purse. Of course, he is also slow, working only bit by bit.

He worked slowly, but it was difficult to carve a small block of wood into the shape of a tumbler, narrow in the middle with the upper as small as possible to keep it in proportion to the base. When he rolled it, it would not stand upright, but remained on its side. After thinking it over, Yun took it to the blacksmith, Big Nose, at his shop below the river bank, to have a piece of iron attached to the bottom. After that, it began to behave like a tumbler. Old Man Yun gave it the final touch by rounding the base and drawing a face on the upper part.

Now it must be taken to the boy. The toy is for Ch'ŏl-hi, the crippled son of the woman from Ch'unch'ŏn who lives a few houses below him. Ch'ŏl-hi is only four, and his legs were paralyzed by polio two years ago. For a while his mother carried him on her back when she peddled bamboo-baskets, but now, unable to bear such a burden, she leaves him unattended in their single room. This tumbler, the old man thinks, is the sort of toy the child might like to play with.

Old man Yun thrust the tumbler into one of the pockets of his work clothes, and picking up his plasterer's tools from the corner of the room, went outside. It was foggy. The heavy mist blurred even the outlines of the shacks knitted closely together on the treeless hillside. He felt as if he were on a high quiet mountain, yet here and there he could hear the cries of babies, the nagging voices of women, the phlegmy cough of old men. Watching the way the fog was moving up the hill, he knew it would soon clear and become warm. Leaving the door unlocked, the old man started from the house and began to descend the hill. It was too poor a house and too bare a neighborhood to require locked doors. He had taken just a few steps when a figure suddenly loomed out of the fog and said,

"Going out to work so soon?"

He was a young man from the neighborhood who had already made his early morning rounds of the city streets to pick up rags. The big basket on his back was full.

"Uhm."

The young man moved sideways to clear a passage for the old man. It was a very narrow alley. As the old man passed he silently praised the youngster for his diligence. We should always be diligent, he thought.

From spring to mid-autumn old man Yun keeps busy as a plasterer's assistant. He leaves for work at dawn and returns home only after dark. From late autumn, when there is little plastering work, he does odd jobs, mostly repairing the grates and flues of *ondol* (heated) floors. He likes such work, for he feels free and independent. The only thing he is sorry about is that he cannot find as much of this sort of work as he would like; no housewife wants her grates and flues repaired early in the morning.

Old man Yun stopped in front of Ch'ŏl-hi's shack and cleared his throat before he opened the door. He always coughed once or twice even though he knew Ch'ŏl-hi's mother had left before dawn to buy the baskets she would peddle during the day. The boy turned his head to look. Beside him was a bowl of boiled rice with a spoon sticking out of it, which his mother had left for his lunch.

When the woman from Ch'unch'ŏn first began leaving Ch'ŏl-hi, the old man would often find the child crying alone in the room. Soon, however, he seemed to get used to his solitude and stopped crying, but whenever he saw the old man looking in, he would immediately begin to sniffle as if in deep sorrow. Today also, his eyes filled with tears on seeing the old man.

Moved, the old man hurriedly pulled the tumbler from his pocket.

"Look here, boy, you know what this is?"

He rolled the tumbler towards Ch'ŏl-hi.

"Holla, holla, it stands, it stands."

The boy turned himself over with difficulty. The old man picked up the toy and again rolled it toward Ch'ŏl-hi.

"Holla, holla, it stands, it stands. You like it, don't you?"

The boy looked at the still-wobbling tumbler.

"Now, you roll it."

After a moment's hesitation, the boy picked it up and rolled it toward the old man.

"Good, very good. See, it stands again!"

The old man again rolled it toward the boy. While they were rolling the tumbler back and forth, a smile displaced the tears in the boy's eyes. Now Ch'ŏl-hi rolled the toy in a different direction. He dragged himself along on his stomach to reach it, and rolled it again in another direction, then in another.

While Ch'ŏl-hi rolled the tumbler by himself, the old man continued to repeat "Holla, holla, it stands, it stands!" His toothless mouth, from which a hissing sound escaped as he uttered the words, was open in a wide smile.

Coming to the bottom of the hill, Yun dropped in at Big Nose's workshop on the corner of the street. He needed to pick up the axe he used to break up earthen fireplaces. He had asked the blacksmith to sharpen the blade the day before, but he visited here at least once a day even if he had no particular reason.

Big Nose was beating on a piece of red-hot iron with a heavy hammer. He spoke as he saw the old man:

"You've had some good luck this morning, haven't you, Uncle Medal?"

"Why?"

"You look happy, you look very happy, Uncle Medal."

"Why, do you think of me as a cry-baby?"

Despite disclaimers, the old man felt satisfied as he thought of the poor boy playing with the foolish tumbler.

The axe had been sharpened. Only the handle remained to be fitted. Big Nose, pushing the hammered piece of iron back into the forge, picked out another red-hot iron with his tongs and glanced out into the street, saying:

"The second one, by God."

The old man, who was fitting the handle into the axe, turned his eyes in the same direction. A funeral procession was passing by.

"Do you often see funeral processions from here?"

"No. They may pass here every day, but I don't notice many. However, that's the second just this morning."

"You don't feel good when you see them."

"Not exactly."

"But you may have good luck today."

"Good luck?"

"You may meet someone you have long wanted to see, or somebody may buy you a drink. You know that old saying?"

"Do you believe in it, Uncle?"

"Not exactly. These days I'd rather see myself put into a box than have that kind of luck."

Old man Yun stood up, putting the axe into his tool bag.

He walked around the streets of the city calling his trade. It was not until almost noon that he found a job, fixing the *ondol* grate in the night-duty room of a business. He worked patiently and precisely. He was so exacting that the employees wondered how many such jobs he could get through in one day. When he finished he even burned a piece of paper in the mended grate. Only when he saw the flame sucked into the flues did he pull a cigarette butt from his pocket and light up. At such moments he found smoking exceptionally satisfying. Pocketing his money, the old man picked up his tools and left the building. He entered the first eating place he saw. On days he earned money he usually ate lunch, otherwise he skipped it, especially on the short winter days.

A woman of about thirty stood behind the counter dishing out noodle soup. A customer, probably a day laborer, stood eating, bowl raised to his mouth. While the woman was preparing food for the old man, the baby she was carrying on her back whimpered once then, rubbing its face on its mother's back two or three times, fell asleep again. The head of the round-faced infant girl flopped backward. Her cheeks were rosy with sleep and there was dried mucus under her nose. Without realizing it, the old man let his mouth fall open in a toothless smile. To him the child was so lovely. The other man, who had now finished eating, put his empty bowl down on the counter and, after paying for his lunch, went out.

"How old is the child?" asked the old man. He noticed that the baby must have been quite heavy, for the stocky mother's waist was pinched in by the cloth band which supported its weight.

"Just two."

Ch'ŏl-hi is four. Now the old man understood why the boy's mother had to leave her crippled son behind.

"You must be tired, standing all day with the child on your back."

"It can't be helped. What her father earns by carrying loads in his A-frame is hardly enough to live on. We must count ourselves lucky to be able to manage at all."

Ch'ŏl-hi's father had been a mine worker who, it is said, was crushed to death in the collapse of a mine tunnel somewhere in Kangwŏn Province. Ch'ŏl-hi's legs were paralyzed and he would be a cripple all his life. Compared with Ch'ŏl-hi's mother, this woman's lot seemed far better.

"You making good money yourself these days?" asked the woman, who could tell from his appearance that he was poor.

"I manage to live one way or another." But suddenly he was struck by the thought that he was really fortunate.

The woman scooped up another ladle of soup and poured it into his bowl, though he had not asked for more.

"This soup is very good," said the old man gratefully as he slowly emptied the bowl.

The day would have passed as uneventfully as any other, had the old man gone straight home. After his lunch he walked the streets a while longer calling his trade. It was quite late in the afternoon when he was called in by a middle-aged man for his second job of the day. He never expected it could be the beginning of something.

It was an ordinary house and tidy, though a little old. He was asked to repair the grate for the room opposite to the main room. The master of the house sent out the maid to buy cement, sand and clay while the old man prepared for his work. As he was raking out the ashes and cinders, the maid returned with an A-frame man carrying the materials. The master called to someone in the inner room to bring money to pay the man.

The sound of the door opening could be heard in the hall. Old man Yun was straightening up to move the bucket of ashes when he turned his eyes in the direction of the sound as if they were drawn by some unknown power. As the woman was handing the money to her husband, she glanced at the old man who was about to turn aside but, despite himself, looked once again upon the woman in the hall. Their glances met. The woman stared with her mouth partly open and she was apparently quite shocked. The old man averted his eyes hurriedly. "Why?" "How? . . ." "What? . . ." "She . . .!"

The old man slowly crouched down on his haunches, placing the ash bucket beside him. He lit a cigarette but the next moment he stubbed it out. He hurriedly collected his tools and sought out the master of the house.

"What!? You're leaving? What do you expect us to do? Why do you leave things in a mess, old man?"

"Sorry, but suddenly, one of my arms. . . ."

He had never lied before.

"Why on earth do you come around asking for work if you're a cripple? You'd better shut yourself up in your room."

The old man quickly stepped out of the house, leaving the complaints behind him. While walking toward home, he repeatedly wondered if he had mistaken her identity. Slowing his steps he thought deeply. "Many in this world look alike." How often he was surprised to meet young men who resembled his dead son! However, he could not forget the woman who had stood only a few steps from him, who had apparently recognized him and who was obviously as shocked as he. It was too clear an image to be easily suppressed.

He passed by Big Nose's shop without responding to the blacksmith's greeting. He hastily climbed the steep alley. Putting his tools in the room, he carried the stove outside to cook his supper. He would eat earlier than usual tonight. At that moment, hands unexpectedly stretched out to help him. The old man's heart began to pound. "It can't be, it can't be!" The old man, without looking at the woman, turned on his heels and started down the alley. The woman remained without uttering a word.

Old man Yun sat with a bowl of cheap rice wine before him in a corner of the tavern across from the railroad tracks. He felt as if an undefinable something were about to attack him. "Why should she follow me? What does she want now?"

For a long time the old man had been struggling to restore his equilibrium; others could hardly understand the suffering he had endured. It was only after he had come to realize how cruel and ugly life was, that he had reached his present quiet state of mind. He did not want – however insignificant he might be to others – to be jolted by anyone again.

The old man closed his eyes and slowly recalled the woman to his mind. She was more refined and plumper than she had been before. Unmistakably she was a good housewife. He could not check the anger rising within him. He could not bear to face the fact that after recognizing him she had followed him. If she thought she had seen an old man who looked like him, she should still avoid him.

Taking up the liquor bowl the old man now pictured her as she had been when she was skinnier but heavy with child. He did not know how long she had been pregnant. However, one thing was certain. The baby could not be his son's. His son had died quite some time before she could have conceived. In those days the old man was almost entirely dependent upon his daughter-in-law. She could barely sustain their life with what she earned. One day she had gone out as usual, but she had never returned. Later he had found that his son's *Hwarang* medal for distinguished service and the certificate awarding a small pension to his family had disappeared with her. This theft made him decide that they should forever be strangers, she seeking her own way in life, he his.

The lights were turned on in the tavern and people came and went. Most of them were day laborers who, having drained one or two bowls of wine, went out chewing a piece of pickled cabbage. Few sat down to drink. Thus things around old man Yun were going on as usual. Nothing was out of the ordinary. He began to feel he was the only fretful one among them. "Now that she is no longer my daughter-in-law I don't have to worry about meeting her, even if she happens to find me, and comes following me for some reason or other. It's none of my business; I don't have to worry!"

"You cut me dead twice today. What's the matter with you?"

The blacksmith came in, blowing his nose loudly, and sat beside the old man. He always blew his big strawberry nose when he entered the tavern. It was as if he wanted to savor the smell of liquor that came floating to his nostrils.

"Nothing in particular. There are such occasions, you know."

"You haven't anything against me, have you, Uncle Medal?"

"Why, no. . . ."

"By the way, Uncle Medal, a dog was killed by a train at the crossing just now. It just ran on along the track with no thought of dodging the oncoming train. There could be no escaping the train by simply running straight on as it did. If only it had jumped aside. . . . Still, it wasn't a young dog."

Big Nose emptied the bowl of wine that the boy poured for him, tipping the vessel so far that the tip of his nose touched the liquid. He rubbed his nose and blew it again. It was obvious he was excited by the sudden death, even though it was nothing but a beast that had been killed.

"A terrible lot of funerals I've seen today. . . . Why, I've seen two more since you left, Uncle Medal. That might've been what got the dog killed, by God!"

Relaxing, he said in a pleasant tone, "Has it ever come true? I mean the old saying that if you see a funeral you'll meet the one you wanted to see, or somebody will buy you wine, that sort of thing? All nonsense, isn't it?"

"If you expect it, it won't come true. You must pretend to forget all about it. Like me today . . ." he was about to continue but checked himself. He did not want to reveal anything, not even to Big Nose, the only person in the neighborhood he could talk to freely.

"Anyhow, I'll give you some luck."

The old man considered he must adapt himself to the atmosphere of the tavern to stop thinking about what had happened in the past, things which were by no means pleasant to remember.

"I don't want you to buy me wine, Uncle Medal."

"Why not? The wine I buy you doesn't taste good?"

He called the waiter and had him pour liquor into Big Nose's bowl. The blacksmith blew his nose several times, but did not refuse the drink. Then looking over at the old man, he said,

"Anything happen to you today? Your eyes look sort of funny."

"Funny? How?"

"They're both red."

A few years ago a piece of brick had struck his

left eye while he was helping the plasterer on a repair job. For a long time the eye had remained swollen and congested with blood. The injury finally healed and there was nothing wrong with the eye now. However, whenever he drank anything alcoholic, the eye became flushed. Big Nose, knowing this, had said both his eyes were red.

"I must have had too much, then," but the old man did not think he was really drunk.

"Well, I'd better go home then."

He stood up. He found he really was feeling light-headed. It was dark outside. At the crossing, dimly lit by street lamps, a policeman was still dispersing the crowd that had gathered after the dog was run down. The gatekeeper, stopping the old man, wanted to say that he could not prevent the dog from jumping onto the tracks. He seemed to be defending himself. The old man simply nodded.

"You're late tonight."

Hearing a woman's voice in the dark narrow alley, the old man was startled. It was not his daughter-in-law, but Ch'ŏl-hi's mother. The old man breathed deeply.

"Well, tonight. . . ."

Seeing that she was waiting for him there, he said,

"Why are you here? . . ."

"You've made a toy for my son. . . . He seems to have been happy, playing with it all day, but. . . ."

The old man leaned forward, fearing that something had happened to the boy.

"Well, a guest is waiting for you."

"What? She hasn't gone?"

He shouted in spite of himself. He stood there mute

for a moment, then turned to go.

"But where are you going? I said she is waiting in the room." Descending the steep dark alley the old man said harshly:

"Won't you please go and tell her to go away?" The old man hurried without knowing where he was going. "We don't have to go back over the past," thought he. "We don't have to! It's better to remain as we are now!" The old man found himself at the railroad crossing. Was it because he wanted to drink more? Not necessarily. Then he heard someone coming up behind him, gasping for breath, but he did not turn his head to see who it was.

"You've become very old, Father."

It was that woman's voice, so low as to be scarcely heard.

The old man walked on without answering.

"I've never ceased trying to find you, Father, during all that time."

A train was expected to pass by; the gatekeeper, carrying a red lantern in his hand, was lowering the barrier. The old man went up to the barrier, and leaned forward on it. The gatekeeper came rushing over shouting at them to keep away; but seeing the old man, he held his tongue.

"At the time there was no other way. . . . Even though I knew I was doing you great wrong, I did it. I thought it would be the best way to raise the baby, so I stole them."

The old man stared vacantly down at the railroad tracks which reflected the dull, cold light of the street lamps. He could hear a train whistle in the distance. What with the accident earlier that evening, the gatekeeper seemed to have lowered the barrier somewhat early.

"How old is the child now?" For the first time the old man opened his mouth. He remained leaning against the barrier.

"If he were alive he would be nine years old now," answered the woman after a moment's hesitation.

"If he were alive?" This time the old man uttered the words quickly.

"Shortly after he was born some officials came and took him away because of the different color of his skin."

Raising her voice a little she said, "Now, Father, you keep this, please. It'll bring you the pension, though it is not very much." She held her hand in front of his face. In it were a sheet of paper folded many times, a little piece of metal and a small bundle of money.

"I don't need them either." The hissing sound from his mouth was stronger than ever.

The woman started to speak again, but her words were soon drowned out by the whistle of the onrushing train. Still, he could gather from what she had said that she had made a new start with a man she could be happy with. The train rattled past heavily for some time. It was a long freight train. The woman spoke no more.

While watching the black cars passing before him, he could not help thinking that she was probably concealing her questionable past from her present husband. At the same time, another thought struck him, that this woman, as well as he, had suffered such hardships in life that it had been more painful, and no better, than death itself. Suddenly the old man was seized with a vision: two people were running before the speeding train; they were running on desperately with all their might without any sense that they would try to dodge it; it was more accurate to say that they were rolling rather than running; at last the locomotive caught up with them. But instead of being crushed beneath its wheels, the train struck them and they rolled on and on like clumsy and incompetent tumblers.

*Translated by Kim Chong-chol*

# Nature

Your mouth was like the shell of a clam, pinching shut as soon as my lips touched it. The soft, sleek muscle inside the rigid calcareous shell firmly contracted, and the shell kept getting harder beneath my lips. But I felt with all my heart that you weren't refusing me.

We were in a dark, quiet park, and you were leaning back against a large pine tree with your eyes closed. I cupped your cheeks in my hands, drew them up, and began probing your lips with my mouth. The warmth from your cheeks spread to my palms. Then you pulled your head down, perhaps to take a breath. There was only the sound of our breathing filling my ears in the chill late-autumn night.

I pulled your chin up and put my lips to yours again. As before, the clamshell pinched shut. This aroused my desire, and I became absorbed in probing your lips still further. And then a soft moan came from deep inside your throat – inside the mouth pinched tight like a clamshell. Before I knew it I had separated your lips.

You remained leaning against the tree with your eyes closed. Your body was tensing, your breath quickening. Finally I was consumed by my desire. I unfastened your blouse, my hands jerking at the buttons, then slid a hand down your neck and inside your slip. You pressed my hand against your body, as if to restrain me. But again, I felt no refusal.

Encouraged, I slipped my hand into your bra. I groped for the sleek, elastic slope of your breast, which rose gently to a peak. But then an odor I thought I recognized, blended with the smell wafting from your body, penetrated my nose. I was seized by a coughing fit. I squatted in a heap at your feet, coughing continually. My long-forgotten asthma had returned.

Mother was sick in bed for several years. Her face and extremities were forever swollen. She took some kind of medicine that made the swelling go down, but eventually her body would puff up again. It was nephritis, but I didn't learn that until later. I was only in grade school at the time.

The man I called Father visited once or twice a month to give Mother some money. He would always leave on the same day he had arrived. He had begun living with another woman.

Mother was a bit over thirty then, but there was already some white in her hair. Occasionally she would ask me to pluck the white hairs. The girl who prepared our meals could have done this chore, but for some reason Mother always asked me to do it instead.

"Do I have a smell?"

Mother would sometimes spring this question on me as I sat at the head of her bed, ever so carefully plucking the white hairs. I would always shake my head. I mean, why in the world would Mother have a smell? Soon the tears would gather in her eyes, and she would murmur to herself, "Your father said he couldn't live with me because I had a bad smell." I was a young boy at the time and couldn't understand what she meant by this, but her words always increased the hatred I felt toward Father and the woman he lived with. But I continued to pull the white hairs, without any prompting from Mother. Until the day she died I never knew what she meant when she spoke of that bad smell.

But when she was lying in a coffin concealed by a folding screen, with incense burning, I realized for the first time that an odor that should have been there in the room had disappeared. I couldn't pin down exactly what it was, but I thought of it as Mother's smell. It was the absence of that odor that made me realize, finally, that Mother had left the world, and only then did I cry.

The house where I had lived with Mother was promptly sold, and I went to live with Father and his other family. Their house was quite large, and one of the rooms across the yard became mine.

Although my stepmother was no better than my mother in any respect, I can say one thing about her: she looked very young. I found out later that actually she had been born two years earlier than my mother. She treated me affectionately, but my relations with my new family were awkward for a while. Long after my stepsister began calling me Big Brother, I still had difficulty referring to my stepmother as Mother.

It was spring when I lost my mother and went to live with my father and stepmother. One day that

summer I returned from school to find my stepmother calling me from the veranda. She had some
watermelon that had been chilling on ice. It was a
humid day, and she had turned on the fan and
removed her *chŏgori*. As I came in she threw a large
towel over her bare shoulders. My stepsister and I
began eating the watermelon. I was just about to bite
into a second slice when the breeze from the fan
brought an odor to my nose. I felt stifled, and began
coughing. I tried to bear with it, but couldn't. Bits of
watermelon spewed from my mouth. My stepmother
rubbed my back, remarking anxiously that I had
eaten too fast and choked on my food. But the
coughing got worse. It was as if each breath would be
my last. Racked by the coughing, I had all I could do
to crawl across the veranda and then across the yard
to my room, but even there I had the damnedest time
subduing the fit. That odor blown by the fan was the
smell of my departed mother, and it brought about
the first occurrence of my asthma.

The second attack came the day I entered middle
school. "Now you're a big middle school boy," Stepmother said to me as she proudly adjusted my new
school uniform. Suddenly the body odor I had
smelled while eating the melon came to my nose, and
again I began coughing, unable to stop. I had just
gotten used to calling her Mother. From then on, I
tried my best to keep my distance from her.

During my junior year in high school, my father's
lumber business failed, and I became a live-in tutor
with another family. I moved around a few times after
entering college, fulfilled my military service obligation in ROTC, and then graduated. I got a job at a

trading company, and I've been living in a boarding house ever since. In the meantime, my stepsister has gotten married, one of my stepbrothers has started college, and the other stepbrother has begun high school. Father has regained control of his business and now he lives comfortably. My stepmother still looks younger than her age, and she treats me with the same affection as always. Sometimes I drop in at the house, and occasionally I take one of my stepbrothers out for a meal.

This was my life when you came on the scene. Who would have thought that my long-forgotten asthma would break out in your presence?

You must have been frightened by my incessant coughing that time in the park, for I could scarcely breathe. And it was obvious from the tone of your voice as you bent over me asking what was happening that you were at a loss. Even so, I couldn't let you near me.

My coughing echoed in the silence of the park. My forehead and the small of my back broke out in a cold sweat in the chill air. As soon as the coughing subsided my head drooped between my legs. I panted, trying to catch my breath.

The cool night air touching my damp forehead and back made me shiver. I looked up. The streetlights visible among the trees were a blurry tangle, appearing at once distant and near. I wiped my forehead and my teary eyes.

You were concerned as we walked down toward the park entrance.

"Is it because you're sick?"

I shook my head, still keeping my distance from you.

"Then . . ."

But I couldn't bring myself to tell you about the origin of these attacks.

You remained silent until we reached the lighted entrance to the park.

"You'd better wipe your lips," you said, producing a handkerchief from your handbag.

Since you don't normally use a lot of makeup, I didn't think it was really necessary, but I wiped my lips once, mechanically. As I had suspected, nothing had rubbed off on the handkerchief.

"Rub a bit harder."

I moistened one edge of the handkerchief with saliva and rubbed my lips again. This time there was something dark on the handkerchief. It must have happened when I got your lips apart and that moan escaped from deep inside you. Perhaps I had bit into your lip and made it bleed.

You once revealed your streak of stubbornness by a story you told me.

In middle school your aptitude for English was clear. You were more interested in it than the other children. Until second semester in ninth grade you always had the best English score in the entire grade. You and your teachers fully expected you would end up majoring in English.

But your plans were derailed by a trivial incident. You had a new English teacher for second semester – a young man who had studied in America. During your first class with him, he said something that upset you. He entered the classroom, ascended the dais, and called on a student to read aloud and translate from the text. It happened that the student he picked wasn't good at English, and didn't read or translate the passage very well.

"Well, people told me this was a third-rate school, and they were right," said the young man. "You children are pathetic, but I feel even sorrier for myself because I've got to teach you."

Resistance rose in you as you heard these words.

From then on, in English class you did everything except pay attention. You would spend the hour reading or drawing caricatures of the teacher with his narrow eyes and the tip of his nose curled inward. And gradually your opposition to him carried over to your work outside of class: you wouldn't review your English lessons or prepare for the next class. You lost all of your enthusiasm for English and ended up in a commercial high school, though you didn't have much aptitude for business. So after graduating you got the job at the bank downtown where you're now working.

And it seems your stubborn streak was also responsible for you and I getting to know each other.

That Sunday near the end of last February, I'd gone hiking with my friend near Tobong Mountain. We'd been to that area often, and we'd taken several different trails. But the previous day snow had fallen – more than one would expect at that time of winter – so we chose an easy trail. We took our time coming down, and on the way we came across an unusual sight – your party of women hikers. All three of you were rather well-dressed, and when I saw your faces weren't sunburned, I figured you had come out hiking as a lark. Since the custom of the hills allows men and women to greet one another freely, we got to talking, and ended up taking the same trail down. I didn't pay much attention to you until we reached level ground, when you and your friends started sliding on the snow as you walked. My friend and I followed suit. Because of our hiking boots we could only slide short distances: we had to take a few steps, then slide, take a few steps, then slide. I discovered that among the five of us, you were the only one who pushed off onto her left foot. I remarked that this was strange.

"Everyone else is pushing off onto their right foot, and you're doing it with your left foot."

"What's so strange about that? Left foot, right foot – what difference does it make as long as it feels comfortable?" You stared at me from the fur-lined hood of your parka.

"Well, can I help it if there are five people and you're the only one who's different?"

"You're quite the expert in these matters, aren't you? And pretty observant too. Well, you're right – I am different. When I was little all the kids pushed off onto their right foot, so I decided I'd use my left. By now it's second nature."

"And I suppose you eat with your left hand?"

"I guess I'd better from now on," and off you pushed onto your left foot again.

About a week and a half later there we both were in Myongdong. What a funny coincidence! You were coming and I was going, and we ran into each other because I was violating custom by walking on the right.

"All these people are keeping to the left. How come you're different, walking on the right?" was the first thing you said. Then you smiled.

"But I didn't do it on purpose," I said, grinning.

We dropped by a tearoom that day. So we began seeing each other, and since then we've become close.

That incident in the park got me thinking.

We'd been seeing each other for nine months by then. We'd taken several easy hikes with the same friends we were with that first time, and we'd all gone in a group to music tearooms. But for a good six months you and I had been getting together more and more often by ourselves. And of course in all that time there was that same odor coming from you. So why the asthma attack in the park? It was just like those times with my stepmother. The attacks I had when I smelled my mother's odor coming from my step-mother were probably due to my latent hatred for my stepmother. But to me you are a world apart from my stepmother. So why in the world would I have had an asthma fit when I was with you? Could it have been that I wasn't accepting you as wholeheartedly as you were accepting me?

Of course we continued to see each other after that time in the park. And, as always, we spent time in music tearooms and went out to dinner and took in the movies together. I was just as happy with you as before. At the same time, what was I to make of this tiny part of me that was on guard against something? I was worried about what would happen if you gave off that smell again. And so I secretly began to worry whenever we sat side by side or took a stroll.

"Your lady's gone," said my hiking friend. He was quite drunk.

I had arrived twenty minutes late at a tearoom where I was supposed to meet you. By coincidence my friend had dropped in at the same place.

"She's very punctual." I was disappointed over not seeing you.

"I told her to wait a little longer. I said there's always a chance you'd be late if something came up. But she left anyway."

"The two of us have an understanding: we don't wait any longer than ten minutes . . . I thought I'd drop by just in case, but it's like I expected."

"Which one of you came up with that loony idea?"

"She did."

"And so this ladyfriend of yours has always shown up within ten minutes?"

"So far."

"You idiot! So what if she's always on the dot. Start showing up late now and then, even if you have to do it on purpose. You're going to have to tame her. You see, men are like nature and women are nothing but cute little animals that live there. Remember that. Now, do you think it's nature that has to adapt to the animals, or the other way around? . . . Enough of this – let's go get a drink."

His breath reeked of liquor.

"You're loaded already."

"Cut the crap. I'm just starting. Don't tell me she's got you upset. Come on, let's go have a snort."

"Sorry, I'm too full – I just had dinner with my stepbrother."

"No excuses, asshole. If your stomach's well-coated

then there's nothing wrong with throwing down a few drinks. Come on, off we go."

The two of us went to a *makkŏlli* house.

I was still too full, so I let him pour me just one drink. He tossed down one glass of *makkŏlli* after another and lectured me on nature and the "cute little animals" in it.

I was thinking about you while I listened to his spiel. All I said to him was, "Are male-female relations that simple? Doesn't it make more sense for both sides to be able to play both roles – for each side to adapt to the other?"

"What a moron! You keep up that kind of fuzzy thinking, and she'll have you wrapped around her little finger in no time. That skirt looks too stuck up and particular. No more fancy theories. From now on you make your lady adapt to you. Understand? You better listen to me or you'll regret it."

The next day we met. I was surprised to see you wearing thick makeup and nail polish.

You saw my expression and said, "What's so strange about a woman wearing makeup? I just felt like doing it. Anyway, what happened to you yesterday?"

I said I was late because I'd taken my stepbrother out to dinner. He was going in the army soon.

"You could have let me know."

"Actually he was supposed to join me for lunch. But he had a lot of people to say goodbye to, so he didn't show up until I was about to leave the office. I wanted to have a quick meal and send him off, but. . . . You know, you could have waited a little longer. What was the big rush?"

"As a matter of fact, I had a hunch something was going to go wrong. And that's exactly what happened – you weren't on time. And I didn't feel like waiting . . . because I'd had a strange dream the night before."

In the dream, you weren't sure where you were, but there was a crowd of people running around. You were drawn toward them. There was a piece of string waving in the wind, and the people were surging back and forth trying to avoid it. They looked like they were afraid the string would touch them. You made your way among the crowd and moved toward the string. But the string kept its distance from you. You told yourself you absolutely had to catch that bit of string that was trying to avoid you, and you were barely able to do so. Up close, you saw it was the line to a jet-black kite that was floating in the air. The line stretched tighter and tighter. You told yourself you couldn't let go, and you held on with both hands as best you could. But then the line snapped. The jet-black kite soared into the sky, higher and higher, as if it would never stop. It got smaller and smaller, but just as it was about to disappear it collided with a star. Both the kite and the star shattered, and together they fell toward the earth. Their powdery fallout was like dark red snow or sand. The crowd had vanished, and you stood alone in the middle of an empty street as the powder settled all over you.

"Sounds like the kind of silly nightmare that a kid might have," I said.

"What's so silly about it? I felt awful with that dark red powder coming down on me."

"You could have gotten out of the way."

"But I felt I had to stay there and let it come down

on me."

"So you can't get rid of your stubbornness even in your dreams," I said.

"It's part of me – what am I supposed to do?"

The story of your dream brought to my mind the time in the park when you wouldn't open your lips.

"What are you thinking about?" you asked.

"Nothing."

"Come on. You're thinking about that time in the park, aren't you? Your eyes tell me everything. In the park I just naturally reacted that way. You've got to understand. But . . . since then you've changed somehow."

"I've changed?"

"Women are sensitive enough to read the expressions and actions of the man they like. Lately there's something about me you've been avoiding – I know."

I winced when I heard this, and I denied it right away. "No, I haven't – if that was the case, then why would I still be seeing you?"

But you were right. I was trying to live up to the level of your affection for me.

Around this time I visited a strange place. There's something about men that makes them want sexual relief when they're restless. I don't know whether you'll understand this or not.

The first thing the woman did was start to remove her blouse. I stopped her, gave her some money, and asked her to buy a condom. She left, but soon she rushed back, rolled up the bedding she'd laid out, put it in the corner, stuffed my shoes under it, and led me by the arm to the next room. She told me to stay there, and then hid herself somewhere. It turned out to be a police raid.

In the room there were two children sitting at a round dining table studying. A boy and his big sister, I imagined. To think that a flimsy plywood wall was all that had separated these children from the woman and me!

As I entered the room the boy turned to look at me but the girl poked him in the side and immediately returned to the book that was open in front of her.

I sat down beside the table and lit a cigarette. The table was pockmarked where cigarettes had been put out, so I took a piece of paper from my pocket and used it as an ashtray.

There was a lot of bustling about in the halls, and then it became quiet. I began to think about where I was. Should I act like I was visiting the man of the house? Should I act like the live-in tutor of these children?

Out of boredom I took a look at the book the girl was reading. It looked like a third- or fourth-grade reader in language arts or social studies. It read, "The autumn weather is beautiful. . . . Our class is holding a party this Saturday, November 15, at two o'clock, as a token of our appreciation for all that our parents have done for us." The door to the room banged open. I didn't look up. Nor did the children budge. "We will present a talent show. . . ." The door slammed shut. "The presentation won't be perfect, but please be sure to come and see the progress that we, your children, have made. . . ."

The woman returned and we went to the other room. But I couldn't bring myself to do the act there.

I thought about leaving, but then I figured I might as well get something accomplished. I led the woman to a room further away, where I removed her skirt and underclothes and had her lie down on the bare floor.

Afterwards I retraced my steps through the cramped, gloomy alley that I had taken there. Strangely, the alley looked even more circuitous now. I checked my watch. There was enough time before curfew to make it to my boarding house, so I decided to walk.

Oh, the emptiness and self-hatred I felt after this mindless release. I thought of you as I walked the night-time streets. Most evenings that I don't see you I play *go*, shoot billiards, and drink with my hiking companion. But as I left the red-light district that evening, you alone occupied a place deep in my heart. All that I had gained from my action that evening was self-hatred, and it even occurred to me that the way things had worked out, it was as if I had gone there to experience just that feeling.

I thought only of you as I walked through the deepening night. In the end, the problem with us wasn't the odor that came from you, but whether or not I accepted you absolutely. I decided that from then on I would restrain my physical desire for you. I wouldn't try to force open your lips. You would have to come to me of your own free will.

I thought only of you as I walked alone through the deep night on a street where scarcely a car passed by. And I realized something – how much I wanted to run to you. "I think I can accept you absolutely," I exclaimed to myself in a low voice.

From then on I behaved differently toward you. I no longer kept my distance.

One night we had some wind and rain, and before I knew it the temperature had dipped below freezing. The next morning all the streets were iced over.

The office was in a commotion as we set up the coal stove. The errand girl was fretting over whether the cold had affected the plant in the president's office. But nothing appeared to have changed. The plant still looked fresh, and the color of its blossoms and leaves was the same. The girl moved it next to the window that received most of the morning sun, and then, after the stove was lit, she moved it close enough to get some heat. But as the heat began to circulate, the blossoms and leaves began to droop.

Outside the temperature hadn't moderated, even by midday. At lunchtime I poured myself a cup of hot barley tea, walked to the windows, and looked down at the busy street. The roadway shone with a coating of moisture where the traffic was passing, but the sidewalks were still under sheets of ice. Those who didn't have overcoats scurried along hunched over against the cold. I congratulated myself on having worn my overcoat to work. You must have worn yours too. Or had you? Maybe you had thought, "Why wear a coat when it's not winter yet?" You and your chronic stubbornness.

While I was standing at the window, a bicycle loaded with small cardboard boxes slid on the ice and fell on its side. Fortunately the rider looked unhurt as he shook himself off and got up, but his load was strewn in every direction. Scattered on the ice, the boxes looked several times more numerous than when they had been loaded on the bicycle.

That evening you showed up without a coat, as I had feared. You walked all curled up, but you didn't complain about the cold, you stubborn little mule.

I discovered something unusual about you that evening. When there weren't too many people around you would slide on the ice. The funny thing was, you were pushing off onto your right foot. I wondered if I was seeing things. But no, the next time you pushed off exactly the same way. I tried it myself. But unlike you, I pushed off onto my left foot. At first it felt clumsy, but then I gradually got used to it.

We looked at each other and began to giggle.

We went to a music tearoom. Perhaps because of the cold weather, there weren't many customers, and we got to sit near the stove. I nonchalantly sat down next to you, instead of across from you. I moved near, thinking I might help warm you up. Maybe I got a little too close, because you stiffened. But I ignored that and kept close to you anyway. For a time I caught a certain odor coming from you, but it had no unusual effect on me whatsoever. I felt that I could relax with you, as I had with my mother. I was overjoyed at confirming this measure of my affection for you.

The temperature in the tearoom was just right, and I felt satisfied soaking in it, feeling also the warmth of your body. But it wasn't long before you wanted to go. There was time before curfew, and I wanted to stay in that pleasant atmosphere, but I followed you out. There would be another time.

Wasn't that weather capricious! The biting cold of night gave way to a balmy springlike day.

At lunchtime I received an unexpected phone call from you. Noise from the street came through the receiver.

"Where are you calling from?" I asked.

"A pay phone. I just had lunch with a friend."

"What's up? We're getting together this evening, aren't we?"

"Actually I have to work evenings starting today. We're auditing."

"Oh brother! For how long?"

"Two weeks."

"Are you kidding? That long?"

"I'll get in touch as soon as it's over."

"Well, not much we can do. I guess the only way for us to talk is for me to call you now and then."

"Uh-uh. Don't even call. When we're busy like this, a phone call raises eyebrows, and I don't like that. So long."

Except for a visit to my father, I went home to my boarding house every day after work. My hiking friend had taken an editorial job with a new publication – a business newspaper – and it became difficult for us to get together. I got the impression he was tied up in helping to get the first issue out. At first, going straight home after work made me feel as though a part of my life were missing, but within a few days I got used to it. Some books I'd bought had been piling up, and I began to read them. I got to thinking that I took more pleasure from books than I did from being with a friend. And so I passed the days waiting until I could see you again.

After about a week and a half I decided to call you

despite your injunction. I knew the two weeks weren't up and that I couldn't see you, but I wanted to hear your voice. You said you'd be busy a few more days.

Exactly two weeks had passed when you called. You were finally free.

You selected the place for us to meet – the Yŏwang Tearoom, a place we had never been. I left for Chongno, keeping in mind the meeting time you had specified. The chill of a genuine winter day closed about me.

As soon as I walked into the tearoom you got up and came straight to me. Beneath your makeup your face looked somewhat the worse for wear. It must have been tiring work.

"I'm haggard, aren't I? Do you still like me?"

"Listen to you!"

You self-consciously rubbed below your eyes.

"But your face looks better," you said with a faint smile.

"Well, that's fortunate."

"Not seeing me doesn't seem to have bothered you."

"You sound kind of cranky."

"Let's take a walk."

You set out ahead. You somehow looked thinner, and at the same time you seemed more grown-up.

We walked some back streets that we hadn't visited before. I willingly tagged along.

"Seems like you've got cabin fever from the last two weeks."

You merely smiled.

It was good to be walking with you after all this

time. I took your hand. I was surprised at how cold it was, and I stuck it in my overcoat pocket.

You stopped along one of the unfamiliar back streets. We were in front of a hotel.

You didn't look at me, but I could see your face was pale. And I felt I knew the reason we had been wandering these back streets. This unexpected plan of yours had taken me by surprise, but I sensed your resolve and led the way into the hotel.

The bellboy led us to a second-floor room, turned on the light, and left.

The far wall and the one to the right had curtained windows, and a double bed took up most of the wall to the left. A cabinet stood against the near wall, and in front of it were a small table and two chairs. A coal stove was burning in the middle of the room.

Instead of looking around, you planted yourself in one of the chairs, reached into your handbag for some cold cream and gauze, and began removing your makeup. After you had wiped away all your lipstick, you again went into your handbag. This time you produced a long, slender brown bottle and some cotton. You moistened the cotton with the dropper from the bottle and set about removing your nail polish. In no time your fingernails had returned to their original color and the cotton had turned red. You moistened a new ball of cotton. The pungent smell of acetone filled the air. You remained absorbed with your fingernails, and didn't look up.

"When I was in school one of my teachers once said that whenever women fell nervous or worried, they can spruce themselves up by putting on makeup and even nail polish – it's supposed to lessen the worry.

I used to wonder what he meant by that, but now . . ."

"What's been going on with you these last two weeks?" I interrupted.

But you didn't answer. And when you had removed the last trace of polish you stood up.

"Now everything's disappeared, worries and all," you said.

At first your lips clamped shut like a clamshell, as they had that time in the park. But soon they opened. The tip of your tongue quivered as it met mine. I was enveloped in a profoundly sweet desire. And I was confident that my asthma wouldn't flare up this time.

I pushed you toward the bed. You offered a little resistance but then yielded.

I had already removed my overcoat, but you were still wearing yours. I began to undo the buttons.

"Just a minute."

You removed your coat and sweater yourself and tossed them toward the chairs.

I slowly slid a hand from the base of your neck inside your slip. You took my hand as if to restrain me, but instead you put it in your armpit. My fingers touched something that felt like a scar. I was puzzled.

"I had an operation."

"An operation!"

For the first time that day, you looked straight at me.

"All that business about auditing the accounts and not being able to see you was a fib. Remember the day I called you from the pay phone? That was the day I had the operation. I had to stay home in bed for three days, and I decided that when the scars had healed I would go with you to a place like this."

"Did someone tell you something about me?"

I felt as if I were being shoved into a gloomy compartment.

"What are you talking about? I told you before that women are sensitive to the least thing about the man they like. I knew you were avoiding me because of my odor, and I knew you had to force yourself to get close to me. And do you remember that dream I told you about? I grabbed the string to that black kite because in reality I was worried about us. I wanted to get rid of that worry as soon as possible, but my stubbornness prevented me letting go of the string. I felt so relieved when the line snapped and the kite floated away. But when the kite crashed into the star it seemed like a bad omen – I don't know why. But the important thing is that I love you. I don't want to lose you. My pride, my stubbornness – it's all gone."

"Foolish girl – what did you want to go and do that for? . . . You just wasted two weeks of your life. I liked you just as you were."

"Why an operation?" I kept asking myself. "I was confident about us. I could relax with you, just like with my mother."

You buried your cheek in my chest and didn't move. The sound of muffled sobbing passed from you into my chest.

There was a sad loveliness about you. I stroked your back. Your skin was firm and smooth, yet rough and pimpled in places. The pimples gave me a strangely pleasant sensation.

I embraced you tightly and set you down on the bed. I caressed you. You went along with everything I did. You were quiet, so quiet.

But then something unexpected happened. I realized that the odor that had come from you before was gone, and I was overwhelmed by exhaustion and seized by the awful realization that my manhood was shrinking. "It can't be!" I chided myself. "It can't be!" But the more I challenged myself, the more my manhood shrank.

I had to pull away from you. It seemed as if black snow or sand were falling on me. I was oppressed with fear at the thought that perhaps this time it would be me wasting two precious weeks of life – maybe even longer.

*Translated by Bruce and Ju-Chan Fulton*

# The Curtain Fell, but Then . . .

– Enter the protagonist! Oh, come on. You can walk better than that. You're not supposed to be killing yourself because you're hungry or brokenhearted. Straighten those shoulders and walk tall. Now how about sticking a hand in your pocket? That's it! And make sure those pills are still there. That's the poison you'll be taking, remember? –

"So you think I'm afraid of killing myself," the man thinks. "No way. Now that I've made up my mind to do it, I'm not all that worried. And as far as my walking's concerned – it's just a habit I've gotten into."

The man walks on. He thinks a bit about the way he walks.

The pavements are crowded with people again this evening. He looks right through them as he walks along – another habit he's picked up recently. The man feels isolated from this endless stream of people. Suddenly, a light flashes in front of him. A photographer has just taken a picture. It is not the man, of course, but a couple walking arm-in-arm next to him who are the subjects. But perhaps a part of him will appear in the photo, the man thinks. From the couple's point of view he's merely an extra, someone with no identity. "So what?" the man asks himself. A bitter smile plays about his lips.

The man turns away from the couple, and a show window catches his eye. He approaches and looks.

The playwright is just behind him.

Various watches are displayed under a fluorescent light. The hands are motionless, pointing at different hours. The man knows it's not yet time. Still, he glances mechanically at a wall clock inside the store. It is not quite nine-thirty.

The man's eyes move to some jewellery next to the watches. The jewels are made of precious metals and gem stones. Each piece has its own shape and luster. The man has never wanted any of these things. They are useless to him. He sometimes wishes he could throw these jewels into the midday sky or strew them over the street at night. What if he could grab a bunch of them right now and scatter them in front of the passersby? With this thought he removes himself from the window.

A short distance away, the man turns down an alley. He passes a few buildings and stops in front of a *makkŏlli* house.

– So you're in the mood for a drink. Okay, go on in. But take it easy on the stuff. I don't need a drowsy suicide on my hands. And what if you have second thoughts? –

"Not me," the man retorts. "And I'm not desperate for a lousy drink."

He goes in. It's rather a large, boisterous place. He takes a seat next to some people at a table. Some of the others are concentrating on their drinking and some are having a spirited conversation. The man orders a pint kettle of *makkŏlli* and pours himself a drink.

The place is one big uproar. Now and then a particularly loud song or laugh rises above the clamor. "I'm alone," the man reflects, "a stray." He tries to forget such thoughts. "But . . . there were times when I didn't feel this way. Like the time I was supervising the construction of that building I designed. I was ambitious, enthusiastic, didn't realize I was working myself too hard, and one day I stumbled on the scaffolding and fell from the second story. On the way to the hospital I felt disassociated from my body. But the strange thing was, for a short time my mind was clear – brilliantly clear. The thought flashed through my mind, 'maybe I'm going to die now,' and I saw faces. Not my parents' faces. The faces of friends who had the same swelling ambition as I, the same desire to do something worthwhile in life. Faces that don't – can't – betray each other. I wasn't alone then. Along with them, I wanted to leave something behind in the world – the tiniest little mark . . . . It wasn't fair to have to die like that. I started crying like a baby. And then I could see my parents' faces, blurry."

The man finishes his *makkŏlli* and gets up.

– There we go! I know you can put away three or four quarts of the stuff if you put your mind to it. But today we'd better stop there. You've got a strong will, all right. –

The man lights a cigarette. And still there's one left. That should do it. He looks up at the sky. The stars are out. "The weather's holding." He smirks. "Does it really matter? What do I care if there's rain or dew on my corpse?"

He feels the pills in his pocket and walks further down the alley. Why not walk around a bit to kill some time? His suicide has already been scheduled. He has chosen a sandy shore along the Han River. No particular reason – it was the first place that came to mind. And as for the time: it's early autumn, so people will be strolling along the river in the evening. What a disgrace if someone were to hear his moaning and discover him. And so he has chosen midnight, the curfew, when everyone will have left.

Further down the alley a woman who had been standing beside a telephone pole approaches him. "Want to have some fun?" He ignores her and keeps walking. Before long another woman makes the same offer, but this one tugs at his arm. "I never knew there was a place around here like this," the man thinks. Several more times he goes through the same ritual, hears the same words. Then he remembers that he still has some money, and he follows the next woman who tries to latch onto him.

– Okay. That's one way to kill the hours. And there's nothing wrong with holding a woman one last time. –

The woman leads the man inside a low, cramped room down a narrow corridor and turns on the light. The bedding has been prepared. The woman stands facing him. She looks much younger than when he glimpsed her in the darkness outside. He couldn't have said she was pretty, but he finds a certain aptness in the balanced features of her small face.

"How old are you?"

"Twenty," she replies in a muffled, lifeless tone.

– Is this trite or what! This isn't the first time you've been to a place like this. What's next – "What's your name?" "Where are you from?" "How long have you been here?" "How did you end up here?" Sounds like a straight answer she gave you, doesn't it? But all she's doing is telling the customer what he wants to hear.–

"You're right," the man thinks.

He tosses his cigarette butt through the open door.

The woman hasn't moved. She continues to look at him.

"Oh yeah, I have to pay her," the man thinks. He produces a wrinkled wad of bills from his pocket and gives her about a thousand *won*, keeping only enough money for bus fare.

She hesitates, then asks, "Are you going to spend the night?"

But that's not why he gave her all the money. And he didn't do it out of sympathy, either. He won't be needing money if he can make it to the river. In any event, he's relieved to be able to empty his pockets. He doesn't answer the woman.

She goes outside. The man knows from experience that the first thing these women do is hand over the customer's money to their pimp. The woman is slow to return. The man wonders if he should leave. "Why not go to the river. So what if some people are taking a walk? I can wait until they leave."

– Good idea. Go ahead. But wait a minute. She's coming back.–

It's a good while that the woman has been away. She turns away from the man as she undresses. "Could we turn off the light?" she asks.

"Why so shy?" the man says to himself. He turns off the light.

He draws the woman close. She is still wearing her bra. "God, what a stupid woman!" the man thinks. "What does she think I came here for?" He roughly gestures to her to take it off. She does so after a moment's hesitation. His hand moves to her breast. It feels taut. He cups it, thinking he has never felt such an ample breast.

"I'm sorry," she says in a reedy voice. "It's engorged. Since you're spending the night, I tried to squeeze some milk out, but it didn't do much good. Please don't be upset."

"How old's the baby?" He continues to hold her breast.

"One hundred days old the day before yesterday."

"Shouldn't you buy milk for him if you're going to be working in a place like this?"

– What nonsense! –

"Milk's too expensive. While I'm out, they give it rice gruel."

"Who feeds him, his father?"

"There's no father."

– Don't you have anything better to talk about? –

After a pause the woman says, "Don't you see? I'm just another case of a woman deceived by a man . . ."

– A "case" of a woman deceived? She must have some education. –

"Then, who takes care of the baby?"

"My brother. He's out of work." Then, in an encouraging tone, "Well, let's not waste our time. . . ."

– Gentlemen don't pry into details. Like she says,

go on and finish your business. –

"I guess I'd better," the man thinks. He embraces her again. But his manhood refuses to function.

The playwright is startled. – What's going on? You're not supposed to be impotent. –

"I wasn't like this a minute ago."

– Then what happened? –

"I don't know."

– The fact that she's a new mother spoiled the mood, didn't it? –

"I don't think so."

– Are you afraid you might not be able to perform? –

"What's there to worry about at this point? . . . I'll just have to wait and see."

The man carefully caresses the woman's taut breast. It is full and hard. It does indeed seem quite engorged. His hand moves to the other breast. Well! It's nice and soft, and less than half the size of the full one.

"That one's always been smaller. And the baby prefers it, so now the other one seems even larger." The woman massages the engorged breast, which seems to be bothering her. "And it's not just my breasts – my whole life's been out of kilter. It was like that with the baby's father. By the time I found out about him, I was already pregnant."

Thus far the woman sounds quite believable. Through his attentive silence the man encourages her to continue.

"One evening a woman came to see me. She said she was his wife. I started feeling dizzy. And when she said they had three children I thought I'd faint. I had to make a decision. 'I'll go see him tomorrow morning,'

I told myself, 'and then get an abortion right off.' I swear. . . ."

The man gropes for his clothing in the darkness, finds his last cigarette, and lights it.

– Do you realize that's your last one? –

"Of course!"

– You're just dawdling here, listening to that sob story. –

"I've still got time," the man thinks.

"I didn't sleep at all that night. As soon as I saw daylight I left my boarding house. I couldn't just stay in my room. I found the place where he works, near Yongsan Station. But it wasn't even seven o'clock. So I rode downtown and back on the bus, and then to Noryangjin and back. But it was still early, it was one of those chilly days we get around the end of January, and I was running out of ideas. Finally I went into a *haejang* restaurant. A couple of middle-aged fellows who looked like day laborers were having an eye-opener. I ordered a bowl of *makkŏlli*. The men kept glancing my way, but it didn't bother me – something must have gotten into me. I'd never drunk before, but I polished off that *makkŏlli*, hardly taking a breath. I remembered the superstition about an owner having a bad day if he has a woman customer in the morning who has just one drink, and so I asked for another one. Maybe I wanted to drink some more, and used that as an excuse. Anyway, I ended up having four bowls. The best thing was that warm glow in my stomach. It felt so good to get rid of the cold. I was a bit unsteady on my feet when I left, but my mind was clear. I walked down the street and stopped across from his office building. I waited there for a while and saw some people going inside. There must have been several other companies besides his. But my eyes were blurry and I couldn't see very well. I don't know whether it was the *makkŏlli*, the sleepless night, or the cold, but my eyes wouldn't clear up no matter how I rubbed them. "That's him," I'd think every time I saw a man go inside. The crowd started dwindling after nine o'clock. I waited quite a while longer and then crossed the street, went inside, and asked the custodian to call him for me. A few minutes later, and there he was on the stairs. My eyes were still blurry, but I had him in my sights. When he saw me he stopped and kind of straightened up in surprise. And then he smiled. I had no idea why – was he embarrassed? Glad to see me? Apologetic? Sorry for me? . . . Anyway, a smile was the last thing I'd expected. Actually I'm not sure just what I was hoping for. I started feeling faint again, and I couldn't see. So I whirled around without saying anything and ran outside. And that was the end of it. He didn't follow me, and I never went back to see him. On my way home I went to a clinic, but they told me the baby was too far along to scrape it out. It was already kicking. I took some Chinese medicine and did some other stupid things hoping I'd have a miscarriage, but nothing happened."

"Is it a boy or a girl?"

"A girl. She's really pretty. I'm glad I had her."

"After you stopped seeing the guy did you ever think about killing yourself or anything like that?"

"Not really . . . but I did have a funny dream. He showed up and started beating me and stomping on me, and then he was stabbing me with a knife. I think he wanted to kill me. But it didn't hurt at all – maybe because it was in a dream?"

The man takes a couple of long drags on his cigarette.

"Wouldn't it be good for the child if you got together with the father again?"

For the first time the woman's speech takes on a hard edge. "What for? I wouldn't take him back even if he wanted to. He has his life to live and I have mine. Before the girl gets too big I'd like to save up enough to open a little store, and then chuck this business quick. But every day's the same old story here – no money."

The man uses his empty cigarette pack to crush out his cigarette.

– Come on, let's can this nonsense and get out to the river. It looks like your equipment isn't up to snuff tonight. –

"Can you wait just a bit?" the man thinks.

– Didn't you just decide to go to that sandy place and wait until all the people were gone? Come on, get up. –

But instead of replying the man once again reaches for the young mother's taut breast. His outstretched hand touches something wet. He realizes it's from the breast, and the next thing he knows he has put his mouth to her nipple. The woman willingly accommodates herself to him.

– Well, I guess there's no harm in fooling around a little as long as you're here.–

The woman's nipple is small, and not much comes out when the man sucks on it. "Harder," the woman whispers. But the nipple on the taut breast remains small, and the man can't suck properly. "A little harder," the woman whispers again. "The baby can do better than that." She props the man's head in the crook of her arm and positions her nipple above his mouth. Now he can suck more easily. Still not satisfied, the woman kneads her breast with her other hand to express the milk. Finally the nipple stands out. At first the man thinks of spitting out the sweetish, strong-tasting liquid filling his mouth, but then he swallows it. He sucks vigorously, swallows continually. The gurgling of his swallowing alternates with the sound of his breathing. With the skill of a mother, the young woman makes the man comfortable as she suckles him.

– Enough is enough. You're starting to look ridiculous. –

Oblivious, the man keeps sucking. His jaw begins to cramp. Still, he sucks with all his energy and keeps swallowing. And then a calm drowsiness washes over him.

"What's happening?" he wonders. He tries to brace himself, and continues sucking. But the irresistible, absolutely cosy feeling keeps washing over him, stripping the layers of impurities from his body and soul.

– What in God's name is the point? How can you doze off at a time like this? Open your eyes – come on. Are you scared of dying? Then let's get out of here and carry out the plan, okay? I have to see exactly how you look when you kill yourself. I have to describe the act in detail. Get yourself together, man. Get up! –

But the man remains at the woman's breast and is

drawn deeper into the trance. His mind clears for an instant. He feels like he did on his way to the hospital after the accident at the construction site. But he's not the person he was then. The faces he saw at his bedside in the hospital – the faces that wouldn't, couldn't betray each other – have been transformed. They're upside down now, and they're planning something treacherous. It was hard to bear. It really was. His rage bordered on madness; a man shouldn't have to cry the way he did. But nothing offered relief, and in the end he became a stray who embraced only despair. He might as well have never awakened in that hospital.

– And that's why you've got to get out to the river. Time's up. If you lose this chance, then everything gets fouled up. Come on, get up, quick! Why can't you answer? Say something, anything. That way you can fight the sleepiness! –

With an effort the man rallies. "What kind of reply are you expecting? I don't have anything to say – I didn't anticipate this, but I'm out of the script now." And indeed he feels distinctly different from the person he was just a short time before. But the difference is not something he can put into words. There is only the feeling in his innermost recesses that this change is nothing to be ashamed of. Before his eyes there appear the watches whose hands were stopped at different times. As they come closer the hands start moving all at once. The second hands move busily. Then the jewels with their precious metals and gem stones appear, each with its own shape and luster. They scatter in waves toward the woman next to him in the darkness.

– This is it. I thought you had some backbone. What's going on? You want everyone to think you're a coward from now on? You want to sink back into those filthy human relationships? Jump right up now, and it won't be too late. There won't be anyone at the river. Come on, get yourself together and get up, quick! –

Suddenly the man is overwhelmed by darkness. He finds himself inside a narrow cavity that is just big enough for his tiny body. He tries to move his feeble limbs. He doesn't feel in the least confined. All at once there is a force trying to eject him from the cavity. He fights to resist. The force returns again and again. The man is exhausted, but he resists until the end. Then he begins to move his enervated body in leisurely circles inside the dark cavity. He tranquilly observes the movements of his tiny self in this womb.

– For God's sake, what a sorry mess of a man. I've had it. Do whatever the hell you want! –

The playwright flings his pen to the floor. Ink spatters everything.

*Translated by Bruce and Ju-Chan Fulton*

# Places of Death

## Place I

I met him in the course of having my present house built. From time to time I treated the construction crew to drinks, to be friendly and to encourage better service. Strangely enough, the chief carpenter refused to touch strong liquor and only sipped weak rice wine, unlike most others in his profession.

This carpenter went by the nickname of "dumb-nose" among the construction workers. The nickname originated from the fact that he had no sense of smell. They say he even failed to smell the smoke when his own house caught fire.

About the time the construction work was nearing completion, I happened to have a drink with the chief carpenter alone. Unlike other times, he tossed off one glass after another of strong liquor, and then asked, "Would you like to know why I can't smell?" His face, as he leaned across the table towards me, was pale in spite of the alcohol he had drunk, except for the rims of his eyes, which were red. Then he told me his story.

"I've been a carpenter for almost thirty years now, and I used to have all my normal faculties, just like anybody else. But one day, about five years ago, while I was working on a tunnel construction, I detected a peculiar odor while touring the site the first thing in the morning, as it was my job to do every day. The smell told me there was going to be a disaster. But I didn't know what to do about it. It was the first time I had faced that kind of situation. I felt a premonition, but I didn't say anything to anybody. I just went down to a worker's restaurant nearby and asked for a bottle of liquor. I thought I'd soothe my nerves by drinking and think what to do. The proprietress looked at me in surprise. Not only had I never drunk in the morning until then, but I wasn't a heavy tippler even in the evenings when I joined the other workers at the drinking table. I told the woman that I wanted drink just because I felt uneasy in the stomach.

"While tossing down one glass after another, I thought to myself that the day shift must have begun by now. As the crew were not experienced tunnel-diggers but migrant workers, they wouldn't know how to escape if something happened. But I heard no news. Then I began to think I could have been mistaken. I hoped I was. But, in another part of my brain, I was thinking that no, my hunches had never been wrong.

"I was just about to tilt my tenth glass or so when I heard a noise outside and a couple of crewmen thrust open the door. They shouted that the tunnel had collapsed. Even though I was pretty drunk, I could still feel my hand shaking. Luckily, there weren't many men working near the site of the collapse, so only one worker got killed and three were injured.

"What told me that tunnel was going to collapse? It was the smell, a faint, unmistakable smell of resin. Of course, there is always an odor of resin around any construction site where pine wood is used for timbers. But this was a different kind of resin I smelled that morning. It was the kind secreted when the vertical beams are borne down too hard by the horizontal ones in the structure, and the whole thing is on the point of collapse. You couldn't tell the trouble by sight. But I was the one who had joined those beams in the first place.

"You ask why I didn't stop the digging? That's what I can't understand myself. It's not everybody who can distinguish that smell, not even all carpenters. So I knew I was the only one who could tell what was going to happen. Then, why didn't I stop it? Maybe because I was afraid I'd look foolish if I stopped the shift and then nothing happened. Or maybe I was afraid that if I got to be known to have uncanny knowledge about disasters and later on failed to predict one, I might get blamed.

"Anyway, I don't have to worry about facing that kind of situation any more. Because, after that, I lost my sense of smell. It just disappeared. But maybe I had also wished it away. Did you say, 'That's very convenient'?"

Place II

The long freight train, with a single passenger car at the rear, pulled into a depot set amidst hills. Several people got off.

A middle-aged farmer, bearded and of medium height, passed through the ticket gate first. Although

old and threadbare, his white cotton jacket and
trousers were well-starched, and over them he wore
a black vest. His gait was somewhat knock-kneed.

The investigators fixed their attention upon the
straw sack which hung at the peasant's side and called
him over to ask what he was carrying in the bag. The
farmer opened the sack, revealing a huge mottled
rooster and a yellow hen. As the chickens raised their
heads and fluttered their wings, the peasant shoved
them back in the bag and drew it shut again.

The investigators immediately thought, "He's the
one." They had received a tip that a middle-aged man,
dressed as a farmer and carrying chickens in a straw
sack, would be getting off the train at a given date and
time. Determined not to let this spy slip through, they
had been lying in wait, watching.

In reply to their questions, the farmer responded
that he was going to sell the chickens at the market.
Ordinarily, he would have walked despite the dozen
miles' distance, but he had taken the train because he
was feeling a bit under the weather. However, the
market day was not today, they informed him, but the
following day. The peasant answered this by saying
that he was unaware that the market day had been
changed. And it was true that it had not been long since
the date had been shifted, with the result that it now
coincided with that of another market. Nevertheless
this seemed to the investigators to be nothing more
than an excuse he had concocted.

Something else aroused their suspicions as well. The
peasant was wearing his right shoe on his left foot and
vice versa. According to him, since the rubber heels
had worn down unevenly, he wore them in this way so

they would last a long time. Although a plausible story, the investigators concluded it was undoubtedly a necessary signal for his contact.

They went off to the village where the peasant lived, and made inquiries. He had a reputation as a hard-working farmer with a wife, three daughters and one young son. Although he appeared on the thin side, his sturdy frame, taut musculature and gnarled and calloused hands all clearly indicated a typical farmer. But even if he were a farmer, they thought, who said that he couldn't become a spy? Rather, wasn't it likely that such a man would be ideal to pull the wool over their eyes?

Although they went to extremes in their interrogation, even bringing him to the point of fainting several times, the peasant all along gave no more reaction than a tree stump. He never wearied of the same explanations: he had come to sell his chickens at the market; since he wasn't feeling well he had taken the train; he wore his shoes on the wrong feet so that they would last longer.

Won and I were drinking at a tavern. He was quite depressed that day. It appeared that someone had made false accusations concerning a translation his publishing house had put out, and he had become embroiled in an awful mess. Normally a man of few words, Won was even more taciturn than usual, but abruptly he had begun to talk of something that happened during the war and brought up this story he had heard about the peasant.

One morning at dawn the farmer was dragged outside. His shabby clothes had become little more than rags and his hair and beard were tangled mats. Since his already warped legs had been bent further inward, he was now limping very badly.

After driving him in a car for a while, they got out at the foot of a barren hill. At that point the peasant, as if only then understanding why he had been brought there, began to tremble violently. He cried out again that he had only been going to sell chickens at the market, that usually he would have walked, but had taken the train because he was not feeling well, and that he wore his shoes on the wrong feet for no other reason than that they might last longer. His voice was raspy and hoarse but he shrieked more loudly than ever. Neverthless, as though he had already realized that any protest would be futile, he began to hobble along the upward path.

When he reached a point midway up the slope, the farmer fixed his gaze on a single spot. He stared for quite a long time. Day was breaking and the morning smoke was curling upwards from the village at the bottom of the hill.

The farmer suddenly collapsed in a heap. He struck his forehead repeatedly against the ground and began to sob. After crying bitterly for a long time, he pulled himself up and silently started to walk again. He was still wearing his dark rubber shoes on the wrong feet.

I wondered whether on that day there could have been another man on the train who was carrying chickens in a straw sack, or if there had been some other mistake.

"Do you think that was his destiny?" I said aloud.

"Don't ask stupid questions."

As if to signal that we should say nothing more, Won raised his glass to his lips.

## Place III

On returning home one afternoon, I found on my desk a book that had come in the mail and also a letter. The letter was quite thick. It was from a stranger. I opened it, expecting to find one more lengthy solicitation for help and advice from an aspiring writer.

Inside the envelope was a sheet of ruled stationery and several torn-out pages from a school notebook. I put on my glasses. It wasn't the kind of thing I expected. The letter was from a primary school teacher who begged pardon for imposing on me, saying that he was enclosing a classroom composition by one of his third-grade pupils. He hoped I could find the time to read the child's composition and added that since my short story "Calf" was based on a child's classroom essay, he dared to hope I might find something worthy of literary use in his pupil's work.

I began reading the child's composition. It was written in pencil on both sides of several notebook sheets. It was entitled "My Mother," and was corrected in ballpoint by the teacher for spelling and punctuation in a number of places. It read:

"I left school as soon as classes were over. I couldn't stay behind to play with my classmates. I had to go home quickly.

"My mother was sick in bed at home.

"My house is far from my school. Coming out of the school, I turn right at the stationery shop, and there's the main street of my town. On this street there is our district office, and if I turn left at the district office, I come to a narrow street. I have to walk the narrow street a long time to reach my alley. At the end of it is my house.

"I usually walk up the steep alley without pausing for breath. But that day, I stopped once. Since my mother couldn't rise from her bed that morning, I had eaten only a little leftover rice from the day before. So I felt very weak.

"I opened the door and went into our room. I said, 'Mommy, I'm home,' but my mother didn't respond and only made a strange noise. I put down my school bag and went near her. She was breathing hard, with her mouth open and her eyes closed, and her throat made a hoarse noise as she breathed in and out. Her chest heaved and sank also.

"I said, 'Mommy, I'm home,' a little more loudly, but my mother didn't open her eyes, and didn't say anything either.

"I shook my mother by the shoulder, but she didn't respond, and only continued to breathe, making a hoarse noise. She seemed to be hurting terribly.

"I ran out of the house and ran down my alley. I was going to look for the kind district office clerk who gave us the ticket for the wheat flour. I thought that kind man might be able to save my mother.

"As I was running, I saw Spotty, the neighborhood dog, running after me. Spotty is a friend of all the neighborhood children. Spotty doesn't belong to anybody in the neighborhood. At first we were scared of Spotty, but now all of us play with him and feed him. We like to make Spotty stand on his hind legs to reach for something we are holding up. We compete with each other to see who can make Spotty stand on his hind legs longest.

"But I couldn't play with Spotty right then. I just kept running. Spotty gave up and jumped off.

"I ran into the district office. I looked around. The kind-hearted clerk was not there. So, I went to the clerk who was sitting at the nearest desk, writing something. I said to him, 'My mommy's very sick.'

"The clerk just kept on writing. Perhaps he didn't understand, because I was out of breath. I said again, more loudly, 'My mommy's very sick.'

"The clerk looked up only then and said, 'Where do you live?' I pointed in the direction of my house. The clerk said, 'If your mommy's sick, you should go to a hospital or to a drugstore. We can't do anything for your mommy.'

"I thought he was right so I came out of the district office. I looked for a hospital or a drugstore. I spotted a signboard that said, 'Pharmacist.' I ran inside. There was a lady wearing spectacles standing behind the counter. 'My mommy's very sick,' I said, trying to say the words clearly.

"The lady looked down at me and said, 'You should consult a doctor about your mommy's illness. I can't do anything for you because I don't know what's ailing your mommy.'

"I don't know what's ailing my mommy, either. I just know that she has been sick on and off for a long time.

"I began running again, looking for a hospital. I saw

a hospital sign across the street. I crossed the road, not heeding a car coming. The driver of the car swore at me. I knew I had done wrong, but I ran on without pausing to apologize. I ran into the hospital.

"There were many rooms in the hospital. I couldn't tell which was the room the doctor was in. Just then, the door to a room on the left opened and an elderly gentleman came out. He looked at me and yelled, 'How dare you come up to the floor with your shoes on?'

"I took off my shoes quickly and said, 'My mommy's very sick,' trying to say the words clearly. The gentleman said, 'Another beggar girl's just been here. I have no more money to give away today. You'd better come some other day.'

"I said, 'I'm not a beggar. My mommy's very sick. Please come with me, sir, please.'

"The gentleman said, 'All right, all right. Here's some money. Mind, don't you try this trick again.' He threw a coin at me and disappeared into one of the rooms.

"I didn't know what I could do next. I looked at the coin. It occurred to me that if I bought something to eat with the coin and gave it to Mother she might get well. I went to the store in my neighborhood. I bought a box of cookies with the coin. I tried to run fast to give the cookies to Mother quickly. But I couldn't run fast. I felt too weak. I ran as fast as I could.

"I suddenly thought of my daddy. Wouldn't it be nice if Daddy were home? But my daddy has gone to earn money. It's been more than a year, but Daddy hasn't come back yet. But my daddy will come back with lots of money. I know what'll be the first thing I'll ask Daddy to buy me when he comes back. It's funny sneakers. I want those sneakers with the picture of the flying monkey on top.

"While I was thinking of Daddy, I reached my home. I had to pause several times on the way, because my legs were too weak. I opened the door and went into our room. It was very quiet. I went up to Mother. She was not breathing hoarsely, and her chest was not heaving up and down. Her mouth was open, and her eyes were open, too.

"I was so happy that she didn't seem to be hurting any more. I tore open the cookie box and thrust some cookies into her mouth. 'Mommy, I've got delicious cookies for you,' I said."

I put down the notebook sheets on the desk and took off my glasses. After a while I called to my wife.

"Was our last-born going to grade school during the War?" I asked.

My wife seemed to take my question as just one more of those questions I ply her with every day on account of my poor memory. She simply said, without even bothering to complain about my forgetfulness, that our last-born was not only going to grade school but was a third-grader in the year the armistice was signed and we returned to Seoul. Then she began to reminisce about our refugee life in those days, but I wasn't listening to her. I was thinking of something else.

## Place IV

The rain which had been falling quite heavily all afternoon and evening cleared up with the onset of night. Stars appeared and the moon rose.

He gazed out upon the moonlit highway from the checkpoint station. "That certainly was sweet rain," he said and repeated it once more. Several days had already passed since he received word from his father that because of the excessively dry autumn the radish and cabbage crops had turned out poorly. Although his parents found it hard to make ends meet as farmers, they never failed to furnish him with supplementary grain according to the season, even sending ingredients for the winter *kimchi* in the fall. He found it an incomparable source of shame to be indebted to his elderly parents as he approached forty years of age, but because he had many mouths to feed and no other recourse, he had simply been obliged to accept their help.

"I thought it would get chilly with this rain, but I was wrong." The young reserve soldier who was thumbing through the outdated magazines on the side table arched his back and spoke. He had been left behind on guard duty after the patrol had gone out.

"Yeah. We're pretty lucky."

The youthful soldier stretched again and yawned. He smiled to himself. It had not been many days since he was married. He looked at the clock on the wall. It was just past eleven.

At that moment a truck pulled to a halt out in front. The young driver got out, thrust open the door of the checkpoint and burst in. "I ran somebody over!"

Thinking that this was the end of their long lucky spell of no accidents, the older officer scrutinized the young driver. The round, flat face, the tiny mouth, the thin lines of his features – it wasn't a face he was familiar with.

"Where's the man you hit?"

"He died on the spot, so he's still. . . ."

The older officer had the driver present his license and identification card. After jotting down name, address, date of birth and so on, he reported the incident to the chief who lived in the checkpoint's rear wing. Then making the driver lead the way, he climbed up into the truck.

"You're drunk, aren't you?" he prodded.

"N-no, sir. I never even touch the stuff."

It was true that the driver neither appeared drunk nor did he smell of alcohol. He was just extremely flushed.

"Well, were you dozing?"

"Dozing, sir? Even if I've been driving all night, I always feel wide awake as long as I've got my hands on the steering wheel. Besides, tonight the moon was bright and . . . I was whistling as I drove. I was coming around a curve on the hill at the right speed when all of a sudden something dark popped up in front of me. I slammed on the brakes and turned the wheel hard, but. . . . No, no, until now I've never been in any accidents at all. . . . He was carrying a full load of firewood, you know, and was rushing ahead without looking right or left. It would've taken a miracle to miss him. Really, there was no way I could help it."

Abruptly the thought occurred to the officer that driving a truck was a difficult occupation. A terrible accident, caused with no warning. . . .

But now they had arrived at the scene of the mishap and he inspected it closely. Astonishing as was the accident itself, he could not help but be more astonished at the strange circumstances which revealed themselves to him. Not trusting his eyes, he used everything at his disposal from flashlight to moonbeams, as he examined the spot carefully again and again. Tire tracks were visible on the wet road where the vehicle had been put into reverse. The corpse was horribly mangled.

He had heard that truck drivers would rather finish off those whom they had hit and injured severely. He felt a chill run down his spine, as he realized that this appeared to be such a case.

"I wanted to strangle that damned trucker on the spot. But on the other hand, do you know what was going through my mind? Not that the victim may have survived to live as an invalid. But instead I thought how the dead man's family could get several hundred thousand *won* to help them out, now that he had died. Isn't it horrifying that an idea like that would come to me so readily?"

The one who had been listening just puffed on his cigarette as though he were mulling something over, and then he murmured, as if to himself, "In the end it seems like he was hit by a truck his own family was driving."

*Translated by Suh Ji-moon and*
*Stephen Epstein*

# A Tree, a Rock, and . . .

*The boy ran about, trying to catch a dragonfly in his net. But the dragonfly always swerved deftly at the last moment, and the boy flailed his net in vain. But he did not give up and dashed about the field, pursuing the elusive insect. Though dusk was setting in and he couldn't see very far, the boy kept waving his net.*

For some time now he had been falling into a strange mood just before fully waking in the morning. A nameless sorrow seemed to brood in him. At those moments he always saw himself as the boy running about the field in pursuit of dragonflies.

He couldn't understand why, after more than half a century, that particular image should occupy his mind every morning. It wasn't even true to life. He had chased dragonflies as a young boy, when his family visited his grandfather in the country during the summer vacation. But it was always inside the village, and not on a vast field, as in his dream. Also, he always managed to catch a number of insects each day. Many dragonflies buzzed around in the yard of his grandfather's house, especially on sunny days after a long rain, so he never had to roam the fields in vain pursuit of them late into the evening.

He sometimes wondered whether this image of himself might not symbolize the story of his life. He had devoted his whole life to studying English literature and had published several volumes of academic essays, but he knew he had contributed little or nothing to the world of scholarship.

It could be that the sorrow that seemed to hover over him and brood on him came from the feeling that his life was empty and futile. Sometimes, the feeling of emptiness he experienced while dreaming about the pursuit of dragonflies clung to him all day, not only on those days he stayed home, but when he went to his office at the university, from which he was soon to retire. And the feeling of emptiness gave birth to another feeling.

It was regret. Of course, everyone is bound to feel regret for the major mistakes and errors one makes in life. But in his case the feeling centred on small, insignificant events that nobody would think twice about, events that he himself had already forgotten long ago. They came back to him apropos of nothing, without any reason for such associations. And they took hold of him and tormented him acutely.

Some of the things that tortured him were such trifles as his having, as a child, hit a struggling worm with the stream of his urine. Another occurred when he was in the first grade. He had grabbed a candy ball and thrown it to the floor when his girl seatmate had offered it to him stuck on the tip of her tongue. During his middle school years, he had bought a pair of pigeons. The pigeons wouldn't come back to the cage at night and preferred to roost under the eaves, so every night he had to grab them and put them inside. After a few days, the pigeons flew away. As a college student, he had made a movie date with a barmaid in a tavern. When he saw her face in the daylight the next afternoon, she wasn't at all the attractive-looking lassie he had seen the night before. So as soon as they had taken their seats in the cinema, he pretended to visit the toilet and made his escape. Towards the end of World War II he was hiding in his country home to avoid being inducted into the Japanese army. One evening he saw a woman of his village stealing into a wheat field. He imagined scenes of illicit eroticism, but later learned that the woman's husband, who had escaped from the Japanese army, was hiding among the wheat. And there were two other incidents that occurred to him more insistently than the others. Strangely enough, these two always occurred to him in sequence.

During his middle school years, he once got a present from a classmate of a royal azalea tree. It was during the rainy season, so the transplanted tree grew readily in his garden. It had abundant green foliage throughout the summer, and in the autumn the leaves fell, like any other of the breed. Next spring, however, when other kinds of azaleas were in full bloom, his tree didn't even sprout buds. He broke off a twig. It was green inside the bark. He waited patiently, but when the flowers on other azaleas had withered and the leaves had come his tree still showed no sign of budding. He watered it frequently and prayed that it would soon come into blossom. He examined it obsessively, every day. But it showed no sign of budding. He broke off a twig again. It was dead inside. He broke off other twigs; they were all dead. So he took a shovel and started to dig up the tree. But when he shovelled away the earth, he saw new shoots on the roots. He quickly shovelled the earth back but the tree didn't revive.

Why hadn't he had the patience to wait just a little longer?

The second recollection that followed this concerned a rock that he had once purchased for his garden. It was one of a number of rocks brought over from Odaesan Mountain, which were mostly a pleasure to look at, with their peculiar patterns of light and dark, or their likenesses to the shapes of animals. Arranged artistically and washed with water, they revealed an added iridescence, and generally gave elegance and charm to his garden. He was satisfied. But there was one rock that was an eyesore. It was a big one more than a yard in diameter, with a flat, circular shape. It had no particular attractiveness, and its surface seemed infirm. It didn't glisten when bathed with water, and was crossed by fissures, so he thought it would crack sooner or later. After trying to put up with it for some days, he asked the gardener to exchange it for another.

A few years after that, he came back home late one day and paused in the garden to look at the trees and rocks. Suddenly, the unattractive rock had blocked his way. He averted his eyes. The rock didn't go away, but asked him, "What was so wrong with me that you got rid of me? You said I look inelegant and unattractive, but do you realize how dignified I am compared with you, growing decrepit as you are with age? You say I don't look solid, but which of us do you think is going to last longer, you or me? Whatever longevity you might enjoy, I will outlast you by hundreds, nay, thousands of years." The rock kept on mocking him, though he kept his eyes averted.

That was only yesterday. Yesterday, too, he saw at dawn the vision of himself as a boy chasing dragonflies. Consequently, he also felt oppressed by the recollection of the royal azalea tree and the rock.

Later that day he joined a group of his students on their overnight camping trip to Yongmun Mountain. He needed repeated invitations from the students before he would take part in even such an informal outing. These days, he always shrank from anything in the least out of the routine.

While the students were gathering wood to build a campfire, he went to inspect a great ginkgo standing in front of Yongmun Temple. It was a huge tree, whose girth must amount to more than a dozen meters and with a height of over thirty meters. It shone golden in the evening glow.

While he was walking around it a strong gust of wind hit the tree. Momentarily, it seemed as if a golden tower had shot up on top of the splendid tree. Then, numberless leaves scattered in the wind. It was a magnificent shedding, with no hint of regret.

Feeling some undefinable but profound joy, he lingered there a long time.

*Translated by Suh Ji-moon*

# About the Translators

**Chang Wang-rok**, recently retired as a professor of English at Seoul National University, has translated a number of Korean works, including Hwang Sun-won's novel *Trees on a Cliff* and (with his daughter) Yi Chong-jun's novel *This Paradise of Yours*. He has also published a collection of his own short stories in English, *Migrating Birds on the Charles River*.

**Stephen Epstein** received his bachelors degree from Harvard and is now a Ph.D candidate in Classics at the University of California at Berkeley. His literary interests range from Hellenistic and Augustan poetry to classical Chinese and modern Korean fiction. His translation of Yi Chong-jun's "The Final Gift" recently appeared in *Korea Journal*.

**Bruce Fulton**, a former Peace Corps volunteer in Korea, received his masters degree in Korean Area Studies from the University of Washington.

**Ju-chan Fulton**, a graduate of Ehwa Womens University in Seoul, received her Masters in Special Educational from the University of Washington. Together the Fultons have translated a number of works of Korean literature, including *Words of Farewell: Three Korean Women Writers* to be published by Seal Press this autumn, and Hwang Sun-won's novel, *The Moving Castle*.

**Martin Holman**, a graduate of Brigham Young University and a Ph.D candidate at the University of California, Berkeley, currently teaches Japanese and Korean literature at Wakayama University near Osaka, Japan. His translations include works by Yun Heung-gil, Ibuse Masuji, and Kawabata Yasunari's *The Old Capital* and *Palm-of-the-Hand Stories*.

**Edward Poitras**, a professor at the Methodist Theological Seminary in Seoul, newspaper columnist, and long-time resident of Korea, has won the Korea Times Translation Prize for his work. His translations include *The Stars and Other Korean Stories* by Hwang Sun-won, as well as the poetry of Pak Tu-jin.

**Song Yo-in**, a professor of English at Dongguk University in Seoul, has translated poetry, plays and short stories and authored *Translation: Theory and Practice*. Former president of the Royal Asiatic Society Korea Branch, he is currently president of the College English Teachers Association of Korea and a director of the Korea P.E.N. Center.

**Suh Ji-moon**, a professor of English at Korea University in Seoul, received her Ph.D from the State University of New York at Albany. Her many translations from Korean include *The Rainy Spell*, a collection of modern Korean stories. She also recently published a collection of her own essays in English entitled *Faces in the Well*.